Dads, Geeks & Blue Haired Freaks

Dads, Geeks & Blue Haired Freaks

ELLIE PHILLIPS

First published in Great Britain in 2012
by Electric Monkey, an imprint of Egmont UK Limited
239 Kensington High Street, London W8 6SA

Text copyright © 2012 Ellie Phillips
The moral rights of the author have been asserted

ISBN 978 1 4052 5819 7

1 3 5 7 9 10 8 6 4 2

www.electricmonkeybooks.co.uk

A CIP catalogue record for this title is available from the British Library

Typeset by Avon DataSet Ltd, Bidford on Avon, Warwickshire
Printed and bound in Great Britain by CPI Group

48754/1

MIX
Paper
FSC FSC® C018306

EGMONT

Our story began over a century ago, when seventeen-year-old
Egmont Harald Petersen found a coin in the street. He was on
his way to buy a flyswatter, a small hand-operated printing
machine that he then set up in his tiny apartment.

The coin brought him such good luck that today Egmont has
offices in over 30 countries around the world. And that lucky
coin is still kept at the company's head offices in Denmark.

Dedicated to the City Lit

And to all the good dads: Peter, Sid, Cris, Jason and Saul

And especially for Asher

1

Blue Haired Freak

I was having a good hair day when this whole thing started.

It was my birthday and, in honour of having made it to fifteen, I'd given myself purple streaks (Blue Haired Freak from SFX hair dyes) perfected using only a tint brush, a tail comb and some kitchen foil. I'll admit it looked fine, but after I crossed the threshold into her front room, it took my Aunt Lilah less than a nanosecond to slam it.

'You're a bit pale and interesting, Sadie,' she said. 'Must be the blue hair.'

'It's purple.'

'I thought you said it was called blue haired freak.'

'It is,' I said, 'but it's actually purple.'

'Well, it looks blue from here, doesn't it, Angela?' said Aunty, turning to Mum for support.

'Enough with the hair, sis,' said Mum. 'I like it, Sadie.'

Mum winked at me. She always gets dead sentimental on my birthday – won't let me touch *her* hair though.

'I like it too – don't get me wrong,' said Aunt Lilah. 'It's a good job, but it is blue.'

Aunt Lilah's a hairdresser and she sort of hates that I do my hair myself these days. She's the kind who still does highlights using a streaking cap. She needs to keep her eyes on her own lid; her roots are beginning to show through.

My family birthday celebration pretty much always follows the same routine. Mum and I go round the corner to my Aunt Lilah, Uncle Zé and Cousin Billy's place, which is a flat perched above twin businesses – Aunty's hair salon and Uncle's Philippine café. We go there every single Friday night and have done since the dawn of time. The difference on my birthday, in comparison to the usual Friday Night Horror Family Get-togethers, is that instead of giving us her extensive opinions on the world in general, my Aunt Lilah takes the opportunity to tell embarrassing baby stories about me. Mum's response to this is to squeeze my arm a lot and get misty-eyed, and Uncle Zé cooks me my fave dinner. This year it's *adobo* – special pork belly and rice,

2

just like his own *tito* made for him when he was a boy in Manila.

'I make it special for you, *anak*. I can't believe you're fifteen. So grown-up. Sometimes I think too grown-up. Much too much the young lady.'

If Uncle had his way, I'd still be in knee socks. He'd be happier if school issued regulation burkhas or habits.

As usual, my nerdy cousin Billy was getting ready to snigger and smirk all the way through my special dinner because he knew that I really hated all the attention. He'd even threatened to invite his band Rock Dove round to sing 'Happy Birthday' to me – the post-rock version, that is. I hoped he was kidding me. Even the thought of a room full of people singing 'Happy Birthday to You' brings me out in hives. Billy did the fifteen thing nearly a year ago and in honour of my birthday dinner he'd perfected this slouching, world-weary look of *I'm-so-over-all-that-fifteen-crap*.

He sat up straight though when my Great Aunty Rita breezed in and sat down at the dinner table. She's enough to frighten the life out of anyone. She's Mum and Lilah's aunt and she also happens to be my oldest known living relative. She's this squint-eyed, formidable

Jewish lady who takes the 25 bus down from Ilford for family dinners on high days and holy days.

'How's my favourite great-niece?' she said.

I'm her only great-niece and she always says this.

'I'm good, Aunty.'

Great Aunty Rita stared disapprovingly, first at the pork belly (strictly not kosher and about as un-Jewish as you can possibly get without being the Pope), and secondly at my purple streaked hair.

'You have blue hair, Sadie,' she said.

'That's purple apparently,' said Aunt Lilah, raising her eyebrows. Aunt Lilah's eyebrows are drawn on with a pencil. I've seen her in the morning before she's done them. She looks like an egg.

'I love your hair,' said Mum. Mum is such a hypocrite.

'You won't let me touch *your* hair though, will you?' I said to her.

Mum just pulled a face at me and shrugged her shoulders. Very mature.

'Do you have a nice Jewish boyfriend yet, *bubelah*?' said Great Aunty Rita.

She always says this as well. I used to think it was

4

funny, but lately it's begun to feel like a test. I shook my head.

'She's only fifteen, Rita!' said Uncle Zé and he frowned at me. 'Much too young for the boys.'

Really, what planet is my uncle on? Lately I've noticed that if boys are so much as mentioned in my presence, Uncle frowns at me.

Then Great Aunty Rita wanted to know if I'd learned to love the cuisine of my ancestors yet. In my experience of dinners in Ilford this seems to consist of salt, chicken fat, liver pâté and pickles (*yeuch*) with a total ban on pig products – rather than the cuisine of Uncle, which is pork, pork and *tsitsaron* (bits of pork). I shook my head again. Another resounding failure.

'So how does it feel to be fifteen, Sadie?' said Aunt Lilah. She popped a pickled gherkin into her mouth.

'Well,' I said, 'it feels pretty much exactly the same as fourteen.'

And thirteen. And twelve . . . I mean, here I was at yet another Family Birthday Dinner. Exactly what had changed?

'I loved being fifteen,' continued Aunt Lilah through the gherkin. Speaking with your mouth full is a given in my family. Everyone has so much to say that we don't like food to come between us and the sound of our own voices.

'Fifteen is a great age,' said Mum. 'You're still carefree, but you can be quite independent.'

Uncle Zé picked up a piece of crackling and frowned at Mum before he bit into it. 'Not too independent, Angela,' he said. 'If we were in the Philippines, Sadie wouldn't be allowed out on her own.'

Uncle Zé was thinking about boys again. He just did not let up.

'Fifteen sucks,' said Billy. 'You can't even buy liqueur chocolates.'

I was pretty sure Billy wasn't really thinking about liqueur chocolates. The first thing he would do when he turned sixteen was open a bank account so that he didn't have to keep asking his dad to pay for his monthly World of Warcraft subscription. He is still such a diehard gaming geek. Albeit one with a true talent for playing guitar, plus a cool haircut – courtesy of *moi*.

'By fifteen I was already engaged to your Uncle Lou

rest-in-peace,' said Great Aunty Rita and she stared at me meaningfully. I never met my Great Uncle Lou, but for years I thought his name was Uncle Lou Restinpeace.

Aunty Rita reached across the table for a fried potato *latke*, which is like a deep-fried potato and onion patty. She carefully avoided the pork. Jews and Filipinos are a world apart when it comes to food except in one area, which is frying. In my family we fry everything we don't pickle, and I like to think of frying as our area of cultural compromise.

So there we all were, the entire family around the dinner table: Mum, Billy, Aunt Lilah, Uncle Zé, Great Aunty Rita, the gherkins, the pork belly and me. Everything was going to plan. I could already feel the hives preparing to burst through at the first chorus of 'Happy Birthday'.

I generally open my cards at the dinner table and this year was no exception. The first card I opened said:

Happy 15th Birthday Sadie, with love from Dad xx

My heart turned fifteen somersaults. One for each year. My mouth opened like a castle drawbridge. *Clang*.

7

This — I was not expecting.

'Who's it from?' Billy asked, peering over my shoulder. I instinctively moved the card away from him. I didn't want anyone to see it so I put it down on my lap. My face felt hot. There was absolutely no way that I was expecting a card from Dad.

You see, Dad didn't really exist.

'Dad' was just a substance selected from a sperm-donor website sixteen years ago.

2

Lying in my Pork Belly and Rice

'Who's it from though?' said Aunt Lilah.

My mouth was still hanging open. I remained silent, mute, schtum. My hand went to my mouth like I was physically going to pull words out.

'I . . .' I said.

'Who did she say?' said Aunty Rita.

'It's from . . .' I tried again.

And it was in that moment of silence that I realised that I didn't actually want to tell them who the card was from. After all, it was a card from my dad, who none of them had ever met, had ever known, had ever had an opinion on . . . and right at that moment I wanted to keep it that way. So I tried to close the card without them noticing.

'Who did she say it was from?' Aunty Rita insisted.

'Who's the card from, Sadie love?' said Mum.

I tried to look casual as I shielded the greeting side

of the card from them, but all I did was draw more attention to it.

'What's the mystery?' said Aunt Lilah. 'Who's the card from, Sadie?'

They were not going to let up, but I was not going to tell them. I held my breath — trying to think of something to say. Someone's name. Anyone's name but Dad.

'Da— Gad,' said Billy, looking at me while I nodded encouragingly. He'd clearly seen who it was from. Luckily my cousin Billy can think quicker than I can.

'It's from Gad,' he repeated. 'Friend of Tony's. We met him at the park festival – he auditioned for the band.'

Billy is one of the smartest people I know.

'Nice of him to remember,' said Uncle Zé and he frowned at me, presumably because Gad is a boy, albeit a fictitious one, and Billy's friend Tony Cruz is also a boy – a fit one.

'WHO ON EARTH IS GAD?' boomed Great Aunty Rita. She's a bit deaf as well as squint-eyed on account of her being my oldest known living relative. 'Is *he* your boyfriend?'

'No, no, he's not my boyfriend,' I managed.

'I don't . . . I don't have a boyfriend.'

I ripped open the next card. It gave me something to focus on while I tried to pull myself together. When I thought no one was looking, I folded the Dadcard and put it in my back pocket, my heart pounding like a hammer. This just could not be happening. You see, from as far back as I can remember, my dad has always been a jar of sperm. It sounds pretty wild to other people when you say it out loud, but it's always seemed perfectly normal to me. I really don't have a problem with the 'unusual' way I came into this world.

There have been a few moments in my life when I would have preferred to have said that my parents met across a crowded restaurant, like Aunt Lilah and Uncle Zé, or that they sat next to each other in high school, like Tony Cruz's parents. But my life didn't start with starlight and moonshine, or even in the back of a Ford Mondeo, like my ex-best-friend Shonna's did. It began with Mum and Aunt Lilah and the World Wide Web. And really, what's worse? Imagining your parents 'doing it' (eek) or imagining your mum on the Internet? Think about it. I know what I feel more at home with.

So sixteen years later, how could there be a card signed Dad? Had he tracked me down? How was it possible? How would he even know I exist? It felt as if the world had more or less turned completely upside down in the last five minutes and the only thing that made any sense right now was the pile of cards and presents before me.

I picked one up. It was from Great Aunty Rita. I knew it before I'd even read the message. It had a picture of some gambolling spring lambs on the front and £20 inside. She sends me the same card every year. The cash prize had gone up though.

'Thanks, Aunty,' I said.

One of the corners of the Dadcard poked me in the back, reminding me that it was still there. It unnerved me and my arm shook slightly as I tore open the next envelope, which was huge.

Luckily, what was inside proved to be totally distracting. It was a giant calendar from Aunt Lilah and Uncle Zé, customised to begin on my birthday, and it was called 'A Hairstyle a Day – One Year of Original Styles'. Each page had a picture of a different style and tips on how to create them. I turned to today's style:

Monday 24th September

Hairstyle: Evening Sophistication

You will be amazed at what a few rollers will do for your hair. I can't think of a better style for a night on the town! It will look as if you spent hours at the salon.

Underneath was a diagram showing how to put the rollers in, what size to use, how long to leave them in and what spray to fix them with.

'Cool present,' I said, and really it was a cool present. I was a bit surprised because 'Aunt Lilah' and 'cool' are generally not friends. Ordinarily I'd have been planning to try out every single hairstyle in that calendar as soon as possible, but all I could think was *I just got a card from my dad* as I went on to the next envelope.

I've always known about the facts of Dad. No one has ever made a secret of it in my family. They talk about everything else loudly and hysterically, so why would this be any different? So along with the embarrassing baby stories, at some point each birthday Aunt Lilah recounts the Internet story – how Mum really wanted to have a baby, but how the Internet was pretty new in those days, and the connection speed was so slow that

13

Mum practically had to get a mortgage out to pay her phone bill that year because of the hours she spent searching on it. And Mum sits there and squeezes my hand and beams at me, and then she takes up the tale and describes how she chose the donor so carefully and how some of the men who donate are so generous.

And Uncle turns to me and says, 'You are all the daughter I need, *anak*.' And then he usually adds, 'And no boyfriends until you're twenty-five.'

Happy 15th Birthday Sadie, love from Dad xx

I just couldn't stop thinking about it. It wasn't possible. How could it be possible?

I opened the next card.

You make me proud Mum had written in her really wispy handwriting. She was beaming at me across the table, like she does, her pale blue eyes already getting misty and we hadn't even had the story yet. I do love my mum – don't get me wrong – but she doesn't half get sentimental on my birthday.

I was in the middle of opening my mum's present when the room started to sort of swim in front of my eyes. I heard my Uncle Zé say, 'Steady now!' at the far end of what had been my aunty and uncle's front room, but which was now a long, long dark tunnel. Then my head plunged down into what felt like a nice soft, warm pillow.

I guess my passing out was what prompted Uncle Zé to bring out the brandy. They must have wafted it under my nose until I came round. That was when I discovered that the nice soft pillow was in fact my pork belly and rice.

'Oh my God!' I could hear Mum saying from the bottom of a bucket. 'I think she might be unconscious, Zé. Oh my God – what a nightmare. Billy – call an ambulance.'

'*Ay naku*, Angela – calm down! She's just fainted,' shouted Uncle. He pressed a glass into my hands.

'Zé, don't shout, please! Now, Sadie!' yelled Aunt Lilah into my ear. 'Can you hear me?' She was slapping my cheek. 'Oh, look now! She's fine. Look, she's focusing!'

'WILL YOU ALL PLEASE STOP SHOUTING!' boomed Great Aunty Rita.

Soon they had me sitting on the couch, while Mum fanned me with her *You make me proud* birthday card.

'Good heavens!' Aunt Lilah said. 'It must be all the excitement. I did think you were getting paler, Sadie, but then it could've just been the blue hair reflecting off your skin.'

'It's purple,' I said.

Mum smiled at me. 'You sip your brandy,' she said firmly. Then she turned to Aunty and said, 'Enough with the hair.'

'I like the hair,' Aunt Lilah shrugged. 'But it is blue.'

I carried on drinking my brandy. It was like sipping fire. We are practically never offered alcohol at home and I could see Billy's eyes shining as the bottle went round the table. He drank his in one gulp, made a sort of a choking sound and went red.

Billy cracks me up. He fancies himself as such a post-rock god, but really, when it comes down to it, he's still a dork who keeps photos of my ex-best-friend Shonna under his mattress.

The silence was almost eerie as everyone sipped their brandy. Everyone except for Great Aunty Rita, who now appeared to have nodded off in her chair, having hardly touched hers. From the corner of my eye I saw Billy reach out across the table and swap his empty glass for hers.

3

Glass Half Empty

The first thing I did when I got home that night was borrow Mum's laptop and update my Current Mood status. I chat on a site called www.girlswholike boyswhoplaywow.com – I came across it when my cousin Billy was into playing World of Warcraft 24/7. I've stuck with it mainly because since I fell out with my best friend Shonna six months ago, I don't really have anyone I can talk to, and I know absolutely no one from my school would ever be caught dead on this site.

There is someone called Groovechick2 who always comments on my status. We generally chat a lot, but tonight, when there was so much to say, she wasn't online.

Stunned was all I put in my status update. I hoped she'd check in later and see it.

Mum knocked on my bedroom door.

'Welcome to the Barbie Emporium,' I said. I still

have Barbie wallpaper. It's a sore point.

'You all right, love?' she said. 'Still feeling peaky?'

'I'm fine,' I lied.

She didn't know the half of it. The Dadcard was still in my back pocket.

'Well, I hope you had a good birthday.' She perched on the edge of my bed. 'My memory is that fifteen is a great age.'

'It's not such a great age,' I said, 'and you have a poor memory.'

'You are *so* negative, Sadie,' said Mum. 'You're not even a glass-half-empty person – you're like "my-half-empty-glass-has-a-crack-in-it". Focus on the things you have to look forward to.'

'Like maybe changing my wallpaper this year?'

Mum sighed. 'Like the important stuff.'

I laughed. 'Oh yeah, like double maths and human biology with Mr Graves.'

I shuddered at the thought of human biology. Last spring, Shonna Matthews, my former best friend, had blurted out the Internet donor story during a human biology lesson. It's not like a class of Year Nines don't know how a baby is made, but for some reason the

19

Government wants teachers like Mr Graves to put themselves through the sheer misery of describing it to us clearly and loudly and with diagrams. Maybe it's a deterrent. If a teacher as unattractive as Mr Graves describes the process of reproduction then the chances are you won't ever want to try it.

Anyway, there was Mr Graves, with the bits of white spittle that collect at the corners of his mouth, telling us about how there's 250 million little swimmers in one ejaculation of sperm, and you only need one to fertilise the egg. We were all basically trying not to pee ourselves every time he said the word 'sperm' when Dena Barbulis blurted out that she was IVF so her conception was a little *different*. Dena's always trying to be *different* – even her conception is a like a giant reproductive show-and-tell.

So then Shonna goes, 'Well, Sadie's mum bought her dad's sperm off the Internet.'

There was this terrible silence. I glared at Shonna. It might not have been a national secret exactly, but I couldn't believe that my best friend could betray me like that – in front of the entire class. Not only that, but she'd betrayed my mum as well as her own. After all, hadn't our mums always treated us like we were interchangeable daughters? My mum had fed and clothed her, cuddled her when she was upset, and Shonna's mum, Jeanette, had always done the same for me. I stared and stared at Shonna in that terrible silence and she stared right back at me.

'*What?*' she mouthed and then she turned away.

Behind me someone stage-whispered, 'Does eBay do sperm?'

And then Mr Graves turned very red and licked the spittle from the corners of his mouth with a quick flick of his tongue. 'Open your books to page 24 and make notes,' he said.

That was why I stopped speaking to Shonna. It was over that and Tony Cruz – more of him later. The point is, fourteen had been unbelievably crap and fifteen really wasn't looking much better. I hadn't bothered to tell Mum about Shonna outing me. She'd just have tried to polish the poo. She'd have found some weird upbeat spin on the whole cringey episode.

'It's all out in the open now and you've absolutely nothing to be embarrassed or ashamed of,' she'd have said, and then she'd have launched into her line about how special I was and how she'd chosen the donor so carefully and how generous some men were, blah blah blah. She would have said that I was being deliberately negative and down on everything. In the end it was just easier *not* to tell her. So I didn't.

'Well, I can't sit here all evening while you moan about your life,' said Mum. 'I have to be at work for eight. Now *that's* something to complain about. Don't stay up too late, Mope-chops.'

She kissed me on the top of my head and then made a sad face at me as she stood at the door. I raised my eyebrows and grinned cheesily.

'I can pretend to be real perky if you like,' I said.

She shook her head and left the room.

I picked up my Snow White mirror that I've had since I was about five years old (almost as long as the Barbie wallpaper) and which screeches at a hundred decibels *Mirror, mirror on the wall, you are the fairest of them all* if you accidentally press the button on the handle, which of course I did. I peered into it like I was searching for something. The girl who stared back at me had dark, blunt-cut hair in a Cleopatra style with fresh purple streaks. An Egyptian queen, but decidedly blotchy.

My skin – which isn't usually my worst feature, being even-toned and olive – had broken out in hives after all. They looked like giant zits. Next to waking up with one of Aunt Lilah's tight perms, acne is almost my worst nightmare. My 'worry crinkle' as Mum calls it had appeared as well. It's like a crease which is always hovering in the middle of my forehead, but which only becomes noticeable when I get anxious.

So, blotchy and crinkled, I put down the mirror and rang Billy's number in a fury, wedging my thumb into the dial key. It rang about forty-two times before going to voicemail and Billy's trying-way-too-hard-to-be-cool message. *'Hi, this is Billy. I'm re-stringing my guitar right now so why don't you jam with me later.'*

So I dialled again and after two rings, somebody breathed into my ear.

'Billy?'

'What – what – I'm asleep. I was asleep.' Billy yawned down the phone. It was one of those enormous disgusting yawns, which ends with a burp. Nice.

'Are you drunk?'

'Yes. No. I don't know. I'm really confused. One minute I was asleep. The next you were waking me up.'

'What just happened?' I mean, I really needed to know because swooning into my dinner had created a bit of a diversion and I'd begun to think I'd imagined the whole thing. Apart from the fact that the Dadcard was digging me in the back – the one piece of hard evidence that something momentous had occurred.

'What d'you mean, what just happened? You woke me up and I was – oooh, I was having a very cool dream. Shonna Matthews was in it and she was . . .'

My cousin's fantasies involving my former best friend were not what I needed right now.

'Did I or did I not just get a birthday card from my dad?' I snapped. 'You saw it. I know you saw it.'

There was a pause and more breathing and another yawn/burp.

'No?' Billy said. Although he did say it quietly and in a questioning sort of way.

'No.' There – he said it again.

'Well . . .' There he was – qualifying it.

'I mean . . .' And then he fudged it. 'You just got a card from someone who signed himself Dad. But it can't have been from your real dad, can it? He doesn't know who you are – where you are. He doesn't even

24

know you actually *are*. It was all anonymous. Your mum would have had some of his details, but not the other way round.'

Of course I knew that. I knew all of that, and I also knew not to go to Billy for some kind of phony reassurance. My cousin Billy is first and foremost a Fact Man. In Infants 1 he swallowed an encyclopaedia and went to bed with a world atlas. By Juniors 4 he was sitting up all night playing World of Warcraft, and since then, he's spoken in a succession of whirrs and bleeps which only he and his weirdy fact-friends understand. Billy deals almost exclusively in stuff you can prove. He is not a Number One Zone of Comfort. In other words, he doesn't always tell you what you want to hear.

I knew all this, but at the same time it didn't stop my heart from literally sliding somewhere down into the bottom of my brand-new birthday Betty Boop Ugg boots when he told me right out that the card wasn't from my dad, and I'm guessing he thought I was a total idiot for even wondering about it.

'Oh,' I said. 'Yeah.'

I pulled the Dadcard out of my pocket and stared hard at it. I hadn't really examined it yet. On the front was a picture of some garishly bright flowers – tulips maybe? I dunno. It was the kind of card you'd send to your nan not your daughter. Even the handwriting was wrong; it was round and unformed – childish. It wasn't what I imagined Dad-writing would look like at all.

It had to be a joke, right? A nasty, mean joke – but who from? There were thirty-one suspects in human biology, but only one who was really capable of pulling such a bitchy stunt: Shonna Matthews.

4

Im Gonna Fnd Hm

My eyes were brimming salt and mascara as I rang off from Billy. I fully intended to rip that fake card into a million little pieces. I would do it the next day. In front of Shonna – after all, it was a dead cert that she'd sent it. During maths I'd sprinkle the pieces over her like confetti. I'd chew them up and spit them at her. I'd . . . I'd . . . Then it occurred to me that if I confronted Shonna with the card, it would be like admitting that I cared, that I wished it was real, wouldn't it? And really, I wanted there to be a chance that the card *was* real because there was always a chance, wasn't there? *Wasn't there?*

So instead I went and dug out the Dadbook that Mum made for me when I was a little kid, back when she used to talk about stuff with me instead of at me. Back before I started being so 'negative' and asking the really awkward questions about whether it was selfish to conceive a child alone or if she should have waited to meet the right person.

'Sweetheart, of course it was selfish,' Mum had said. 'Having more children on this planet is totally selfish – but that's with one parent *or* with two. It's never about *needing* children, it's about *wanting* them. The point is that I wanted you, darling. If I'd waited for the "right person", you just wouldn't have made it here at all. There are no "right people" in my experience – well, your Aunt Lilah got him.'

I can sort of see her point. On the evidence of the two dates she's had in the past fifteen years (the ones I know about) I'm jumping for joy that neither is my dad. To conceive a kid with either of those goobers would have definitely been more selfish than carefully selecting someone from a database of generous donors.

Eventually Mum and I stopped talking about this stuff and now we just have walk-on roles in Aunt Lilah's version of events every birthday instead. Now we don't really talk at all.

There is only one photo of Dad in the Dadbook. It's of him as a baby and he's just like this generic baby – y'know? Winston Churchill Baby with a bit of blond fuzz and a face like a potato. I sometimes wonder whether it isn't really a picture of my dad at all but just a photo of Any Baby. Because Winston Churchill Baby certainly doesn't look anything like Sadie Baby. I'm very small, even when I was born, and I have dark skin like Mum, although she has pale blue eyes and mine are brown like Billy's. I had lots of dark curly hair then. I still have dark hair, although nowadays it's straight like Uncle's.

I used to stare and stare at that picture of Dad when I was younger, maybe hoping against hope that I would see some resemblance that might mean I was like him. Because that would make me all unknown and different, not hysterical and argumentative and embarrassing like Mum and her family. I mean, I love my family and all that, but there are moments when I can't be in the same room as them for longer than five minutes without wanting to kill them all one by one very slowly. And outside of the room it's even worse. I mean, in public.

Have you ever become aware of the fact that the people making more noise than anyone else in the train carriage are *your* family? Or that the people in the restaurant with the most allergies and food intolerances and just plain fussiness are *your* family? Some people say that a family is just a bunch of people who eat food together, but hate each other. On the worst Friday evenings I can see there's something in that.

I turned to the page where I keep the Dad essay – something the sperm bank made him write some sixteen years ago, about the reasons why he wanted to make his 'contribution'. Sometimes I would spend half an hour looking at that photo and rereading the essay. I read it again now.

This is a little weird – like writing a love letter to someone you've never met. Don't worry, I'm not going to get deep and hand out pearls of wisdom. I'm not nearly old enough or wise enough for that game yet. If you're reading this then you're interested in who your biological father is, I guess. Well, it's me, and one of the main reasons I wanted to do this is because someone close to me had problems having children and it got me thinking about how many people want and deserve kids around the world, but can't have them.

I hope you've had a great life so far. I'm sure you realised something long ago that I've only just figured out – that life is very long and very strange and very wonderful. I'm proud to

have contributed in some way to giving you life and to help
create a new family with people who will love and care for you.
Enjoy this amazing world.'

It's pathetic really, but there have been moments
when I've come home from school and read that note
and buried my head in it and cried – like the time after
Mr Graves's human biology lesson. Don't ask me why.
It's not like the man is saying anything profound or
personal. It's just that the note tells me that the person
with whom I share my genetic inheritance is real and
not just stuff in a test tube. And if Billy is right and the
birthday card isn't real, well, that doesn't change the
fact that I do have a biological dad out there somewhere.
A dad who wrote that essay and who's never even met
my Aunt Lilah or been scared half to death by my Great
Aunty Rita. A dad who gave me something of his and
didn't give it to anyone else in my family.

And then I knew exactly what I was going to do next
so I texted Billy.

SD: Im gonna fnd hm
Billy: Wot

SD: I'm going to find him

Billy: Who

SD: My dad Who do u think?

Billy: Cool (;

ZZZZZZZZZZZZZZZZZZZZZZZZZZZZZZZZZZZZZZ

Finally, feeling a bit better, I got out Mum's laptop and checked the net. Groovechick2 was online. I was glad to see her.

Current Mood: Stunned

Groovechick2: Wossup?

SayD: Got a b-day card from my dad

Groovechick2: Thought you never had a dad

SayD: I don't – that's y I'm STUNNED

Groovechick2: Think some1s pranking u?

SayD: Yuh-huh. Really upset. Bad enuff that people no my damage at skool without this 2

Groovechick2: Hv u told any1 about the card?

SayD: No. Can't. Well my cousin knows but that's it

Groovechick2: Y not?

SayD: I want 2 keep it 2 myself. I don't want them all in my face.

32

Groovechick2: Wot u gonna do?

SayD: Im gonna fnd hm. My dad. I'm gonna find my dad

Groovechick2: Good 4 u

SayD: He's out there somewhere – so now I'm gonna find him even if it's just to spite whoeva sent that card

Groovechick2: Woz it the meangirlz?

SayD: What do u think?

Groovechick2: They r real mean

5

Shonna Matthews Hates Me

Tuesday 25th September
Hairstyle: Gorgeous Prom Hair with a sleek flip or ringlet
You need to give this plenty of volume from below so that
the flip or ringlet holds up. Tease the hair down to the root
from underneath and use styling spray on the ends. Then
curl up with a metal round brush while blow-drying or put
in a roller for a ringlet. You're picture-perfect! Hold on to
that good feeling.

It was the day after the Dadcard and my fifteenth
birthday. More importantly it was the day after I decided
to find my dad and I woke up to a really fine morning.
Sunshine was peeping through my blind, casting bright
stripes across my so-lame-it's-starting-to-be-ironic
Barbie wallpaper. I felt really fresh and new, like life was
this crisp blank page. Just for a few seconds. Until I
remembered I had to face school and Shonna Matthews.

34

A year ago I would have raced to school and shown Shonna the Dadcard. I probably would have texted her from the birthday dinner table, right before I swooned into my food, and she would've texted me straight back. She would've said something like, '*And that's news? What wig is your Aunty Rita wearing? Now that's what I call news.*' Because she's like that, Shonna — she's sarcastic. People think she's hard, but she just thinks everything's a laugh, that's all.

Except a year ago there wouldn't have been a Dadcard because I was 99.9 per cent sure that the card was my former best friend's handiwork.

Since Shonna and I stopped speaking, I don't have any friends. I'm kind of shy at making friends because I've never really had to. You see there's always been Shonna and any other friends I ever had were through her. Since we broke up, they've drifted away. It's not like I can go and crash some other clique. By Year Ten your friends are made, so now I don't have any at all, apart from Groovechick2 and I don't even know where she lives.

Hell, I don't even know if Groovechick2 is actually a 'she'. I mean, maybe she's a forty-five-year-old guy pretending to be a WoW widow so he can chat up the rest of us online losers. It doesn't really matter. It's not as if I'm ever gonna meet Groovechick2. I just wanna talk to her online. Meanwhile, in the real world, I spend my school days trying not to run into Shonna or any of her cronies.

After breakfast, I opened my calendar at today's style and perfected my Prom Hair with Flip. It looked pretty cool – I think it was the straightening serum I used before I curled the ends. When Shonna and I were best friends, we'd spend hours styling each other's hair. The first style we perfected was the French plait – that was in Juniors 3 and it started a huge trend which went right up and down the school.

I have to be honest and say that I am the talented one where hairstyling is concerned. Since we stopped speaking, I've noticed Shonna has had a lot of bad hair days that I could have helped her with. I, on the other hand, try to be experimental with my hair, which means I get told I look like a cross between Wednesday Addams and Emily the Strange by that Oracle of Style, Aunt Lilah.

I do want to be a hairdresser when I leave school,

but not a hairdresser like her. I don't want to be giving my customers bubble perms or 'Rachels' or any other hairdo that actually bit the radish twenty years ago.

The Prom Hair with Flip didn't have staying power as it turned out. It wouldn't have even made it through a car journey to a prom. It lasted about as long as my faintly good feeling and by the time I reached first lesson, double maths, I knew I was going to have to find a more radical styling spray because the 'flip' had drooped along with my mood.

They were standing in front of the maths room, Shonna and her new best friend Imelda. They saw me and smiled at one another like they were sharing some hilarious secret joke. The Dadcard? I put my head down and tried to look small (which is not that hard for me – have you ever seen plankton trying to look small?). I tried to keep calm – *breathe in; breathe out* – but my hands were shaking like they had at the dinner table the night before and I had to plunge them into my pockets to stop them.

As I went by, someone stuck out her foot and next thing I was on my face – not in a soft pillow of my dinner this time, but slap bang on the floor in the maths room. I'd hit my teeth and I could see drops of blood as I stood up.

Kip came over. Kip is Class Nice Boy.

'You OK?' he said.

I could taste blood on my lips and it was on the back of my hands where I tried to wipe it off. It was on my maths book too.

'No,' was all I said.

I heard someone snigger behind me. Shonna? Imelda?

I was trying really very hard not to cry because there is nothing worse than crying in front of your former best friend who hates you. So I sat on a desk and concentrated on the whiteboard at the front of the class, which showed an explanation of simultaneous equations:

$$2x + y = 7$$
$$3x - y = 8$$

By the time I'd worked out that $x = 3$ and $y = 1$, I'd almost conquered the urge to cry. The tears stayed in their ducts. My mouth was still dripping blood though. It was pretty dramatic. It was like I was doing some kind of weird vampire impersonation in the middle of class.

There was a commotion behind me as Mr Stone appeared through the door, all concerned and flappy and five minutes late. Mr Stone is always late – if he'd just been on time and watching what was going on, Shonna and Imelda wouldn't have been able to trip me in the first place.

'You should go to sick bay,' he said when he saw the blood. 'Here – Shonna will take you, won't you?' He grabbed Shonna as she tried to slink by to her seat.

'Yes, sir,' she said, and shot me this look like I was dead meat. She really, really hates me.

I guess Mr Stone still thinks me and Shonna are best mates. But we aren't. I hate her and she hates me. It's a really simple equation. The thing is I still can't quite work out how we went from one simple equation to another:

Shonna + Sadie = Best Mates

(Shonna)x + Sadie = Worst Enemies

I guess Imelda = x

Anyway, Shonna and I left the room together and headed down the corridor. I glanced up at her. Her stoopid beehive updo was looking extra ratty. Good.

'What did I do?' she said, catching my gaze – like

she was a nice kid, like she was my best friend again.

'You hurt me,' I said and blood dripped from my mouth on cue. I was staring at her and I was wishing that she'd just turn to me like she used to when we argued, and say, '*Oh whatever – it's not terminal,*' and start laughing, and then we'd both be in hysterics, like you just are half the time with your best friend.

Instead she looked at me and said, 'I didn't hurt you – you tripped. But you can blame me if you want to, you freak.'

She dumped me at the sick bay door and stormed off. I guess she was going for a smoke behind the bins before heading back to maths. She stinks of fags since she started hanging out with Imelda.

I went in and sat in the rubber chair, feeling as miserable as the room. There wasn't much the nurse could do for me. It was just a fat lip and a chipped tooth. A cold compress and an appointment to make with the dentist.

By lunchtime the fat lip was starting to go down. I ventured to my locker to retrieve my sandwiches and then headed to the music lab to find Billy. That's where his band hung out – Billy, his band and Tony Cruz.

6

A Short Aside on Haironomics

The only reason Tony Cruz – who is Mr High School Cutie of the Year – ever agreed to be in my cousin Billy's band was because I totally sorted Billy's hair. I mean, I believe they were acquainted before my scissors did their magic, seeing as they bonded over the post-rock scene and their love of guitars and all, but the haircut really sealed the deal. If they had Expertise ratings for styling, like they do for World of Warcraft, I'd be like level 60.

I have it all figured out – how styling works. Not just for Billy, but for all people in search of a decent haircut.

Let me give you a bit of background on my aunt's salon and then I'll introduce you to my Hairdressing Economic Theory. My Aunt Lilah's full name is Delilah and her salon is unironically named after her. That's right – the salon is called Delilah's. That's the character in the Bible who took away her husband's strength along with his hair. Need I go on?

In my opinion, the name isn't the only thing that's wrong with Delilah's. It's not a massively successful salon. Don't get me wrong – Aunt Lilah can cut hair and all, and she has a longish list of loyal clients who she waves and straightens on a regular basis. But after twenty-five years in the biz, she still hasn't discovered basic hairdresser economics. If she had, it could have taken her to the next level in World of Hairdressing.

Put it this way: if you asked anyone to name the most popular hairstyle of the last decade, they'd probably say the bob or maybe the pixie. Certainly those are the most famous. But what people don't seem to realise is that the most *popular* style for women is still Long Hair. People think that more working women = more short haircuts, but personally I think that's rubbish. In fact, I know it's rubbish.

Short hair needs more preening to look good. To look feminine with short hair, you've got to pile on the make-up and, more importantly, you've got to make time to go to the hairdresser. Long hair, on the other hand, is automatically feminine – unless you go for the centre-parted, greasy hippy look – and you can pile it up if it needs a wash, and you don't have to visit a hairdresser for months on end.

Well, Aunt Lilah is always encouraging her clients to stick with their long tresses, but I've worked out that if hairdressers want to make money – if they want to take it to the next level – then they've got to get women to go short. There is no alternative. The 1980s must have been boom time for hairdressers because all the women had short hair and power bobs, and even if their hair was long, it was permed to death.

I haven't even started my career yet and I've sussed this out. I just know I'm going to make level 80 as a hairdresser because I already understand hair, and not just how to cut it. You've got to create a style that looks great, but which is labour-intensive and can only be done *in* the salon, not at home in front of the telly.

Two summers ago in Careers 8, Shonna and I did a business model for our salon Hair Brain. I was chief stylist and Shonna did the finances and ran the show. Like I said, Shonna can't do hair for toffee, but she's pretty good at getting people to like her. She does this thing with boys where she talks really quietly so that they have to lean forward. *'It works every time, Sadie — you should try it. You talk quiet and they lean down towards you and they stare at your lips and the next thing you know . . .'*

Anyway, she was totally perfect for front of house. Billy was our first 'client' because of course Shonna didn't have any problem getting Billy to like her. My cousin still has pictures of her wearing her Dorothy costume from last year's school production of *The Wizard of Oz* hidden under his mattress. And he thinks I don't know.

So we totally sorted his hair, which was greasy and dry and lank and curly all at the same time.

Do not underestimate the transformative power of a stylish haircut. This one acted like mutagen. My cousin became a new man overnight just like the turtles became Ninjas. He stopped going to bed with the world atlas and sitting up late playing World of Warcraft, and concentrated on learning everything there was to know about electric guitars and how to play them. So then he and Tony Cruz became bezzie mates — in so far as boys who have a tendency to whirr and bleep at each other can have best mates. They said things like 'watch that G chord' or 'A minor, dude'. And suddenly Billy had the band that everyone wanted to be in, and Tony Cruz became the lead singer that every girl wanted to snog.

I can't take credit for all of it, but I do have the power. That's all I'm saying.

I'm pretty sure that most of the girls at my school are in lurve with Tony Cruz or think he's hot, but Shonna Matthews, who was my best friend since primary – since pre-school! – always really loved him a lot. She loved him the most. But the irony is that since I stopped speaking to Shonna over her outing me as Donor Girl of the Year, I've ended up hanging out with Tony Cruz more and more to get away from her. And I think it must pee her off big time.

Tony Cruz Who's Hot But Nods Way Too Much

On my way to the music lab I had to pass Shonna and Imelda by the library steps. There are two thousand kids in my school, but somehow I always manage to bump into those two. They stared at me and then Imelda called out, 'Happy Birthday, Sadie!'

And then I heard Shonna telling Imelda to shut up. My scalp prickled underneath my long, sexy Prom Hair with Flip, which now lay flat against my scalp. I tried to picture the handwriting in the Dadcard again. Was it Shonna's? Imelda's even? *Would* they? Of course they would. Who was I kidding? I yanked open the heavy door to the music lab.

The school music labs are well soundproofed, so when you walk in on a rehearsing band, it's pretty extreme. The noise hit me like a tidal wave, as did the smell. It was hot and stuffy and it smelled of boys and sweat and half-eaten sandwiches. All five members of Rock Dove (a frankly sad and tragic name) were there, thrashing guitars and yelling about bpm and 'too much bass here' and 'not enough hi-hat there'.

'Hey, Sadie,' said Tony as I walked in, trying to hide my fat lip under my 'flip'. 'How's it feel to be fifteen?' He put down his guitar and walked over to me.

I fought off Total Boy Paralysis, which is something that happens when cute boys talk to me. I opened my school bag and started rummaging inside it for something . . . anything! I just needed something to focus on that wasn't Tony Cruz.

'Hey, Tony,' I forced myself to say as casually as I could, while casually hunting in my casually opened school bag. 'So far fifteen is a bit like being fourteen with an extra candle.'

Was that OK? Did I just sound like a wacko?

He laughed. I guess what I said wasn't too freaky, although I was sure my face would betray me and I'd start breaking out in hives. I already felt hot. How do girls do this – have conversations with boys? Especially boys who everyone fancies.

There is no denying the fact that Tony Cruz is the

best-looking kid in my school and I couldn't help getting a kick out of his knowing my name, let alone trying to start a conversation with me. He's very tall and athletic – when he's not in the band he's scoring goals and shooting baskets (*so* not my type) – and he has dark hair with what my Aunt Lilah would call 'natural movement'. Tony's eyes are a cool blue and he has a surprisingly girly mouth, which has a little scar above the top lip, and then this square jaw like a superhero in one of Billy's graphic novels.

But I've noticed this one thing that Tony Cruz does that I am just not that sure about. It's a nodding thing. He nods about everything.

'Yeah, yeah, that's cool, Billy, man,' he'll say, his head bobbing up and down. 'No, no, no, that is not cool,' he'll say about something else, but still the nodding thing's going on.

It gives him this air of amazing positivity, but I just keep thinking of those dogs in the back of cars driven by people like Uncle Zé's cousin Moss, who gave up work to do eBay. He had a Tony-Cruz-nodding-head dog in the back of his car, and his wife left him last year because she couldn't stand being married to someone who did eBay for a living. Before she left she decapitated the nodding dog.

So anyway, then Billy switched off his amp and came over and we started to chat. Firstly about my falling over in maths — because that's what I decided I would tell everyone, that I tripped and fell. I can't work out if this was because I didn't want to give Imelda and Shonna the satisfaction of knowing that they were getting to me, or because I was scared of what they'd do if I told tales. Whatever. I was on a roll and actually enjoying gabbing to Tony Cruz, although in my head the whole time I kept thinking, *You're having a conversation with Tony Cruz you're having a conversation with Tony Cruz you're having a conversation with Tony Cruz*, which made it difficult to concentrate.

I watched his cute little head bob up and down and so then I talked about my birthday and my Betty Boop Uggs that Mum gave me, and before I knew what I was even saying I whispered, 'I also got a card from my dad!'

I bit down hard on my fat lip and it stung like hell. I had to stop myself from screaming out in pain. I don't know why I mentioned the Dadcard — maybe it was just to rekindle the good feeling I'd woken up with that morning when the sun was shining.

Tony's eyebrows shot to the top of his head and he moved closer to me and Billy, lowering his voice so that no one else could hear what we were saying. All the while his head was nodding away like it was going to fall off. 'Wow, that must have been a helluva surprise for you all!' Nod. Nod. Nod.

'Yeah. But only me and Billy know about it.'

'Oh!' goes Tony, looking over at Billy. 'OK.' His head was still waggling. 'You guys keeping it secret?'

'Yup,' Billy said, raising his eyebrows. 'The card isn't real anyway.'

That's right, Billy. Burst my balloon all over again, why don't you?

'But even if it isn't,' I said, 'it's definitely got me thinking about finding my dad. I mean, I'm pretty determined to search on my own. Well, maybe with Billy's help.'

And then Tony said something that made me stop noticing the head thing quite so much.

'Good idea. Your family'll just take it over if you give them half a chance. Specially Billy's ma – you know what I'm saying?'

50

'Yes,' I said. 'I do.' And I was genuinely touched for just a second because this was a smart observation. Aunt Lilah's lack of subtlety was clearly famous across five continents.

Then one of the other boys in the band came in with a great clanging guitar chord and Billy said something about frets, and he and Tony started whirring and bleeping at each other. I felt totally dismissed and my face got hot again, so I went and sat in the corner and made a start on my homework. I resolved not to notice how blue Tony Cruz's eyes were, or how cute his little head was bobbing about, or how he leaned when he sang with the band.

I needed Groovechick2's take on all of this, so when I got home I checked out the net.

Current Mood: I like this guy who nods

Groovechick2: Hey SayD - who's the guy who nods?
SayD: This guy. Who nods. Nodding guy
Groovechick2: Is he a WoW guy?
SayD: No! He coooool. I thought I didn't like him, but now I

realise I do. D'you think he'll like me back?

Groovechick2: Sure sure he will – why wouldn't he?

SayD: Because I'm short and I'm shy & I have no friends & my hands shake when I'm nervous and I break out in hives

Groovechick2: Is there anything good about you, SayD?

SayD: I do good hair

Groovechick2: I bet ur fit. Hairdressers always look good. It's just the meangirlz who don't like u, & who cares about them?

SayD: He will neva like me bak. I just know it. How do I get him to like me bak?

Groovechick2: Be yourself. No games. How are those meangirlz at skool?

SayD: Mean

Groovechick2: U need 2 go get em

SayD: 2 scared

Groovechick2: Don't b. Remember ur way betta than them

8

I Have No Y Chromosomes

I closed down Mum's laptop and went into my bedroom, carefully shutting the door to the Barbie Emporium. I needed some time to myself. I needed to process what had happened since my birthday, and I needed to do it alone. I didn't want Mum popping her head round for one of her 'little chats' when she got back from work. Tony Cruz was quite right — the Dadcard was *my* information, and sharing it with my family felt so wrong.

I could just imagine Mum's take on it if I told her I wanted to contact my dad. She'd get all overanxious and neurotic. She'd wonder whether she was lacking in the parental department. You see, even though Mum had always said she'd help me trace my dad when the time was right, I suspected that the time would never feel 'right' to her. Of course, I've asked her outright for details about my dad. I used to do it all the time when I was a kid. She says that she's given me every scrap of info she has, which is basically everything that is in the Dadbook: Winston-Churchill-Baby photo + essay.

So if I told her about the Dadcard and how it had inspired me to search for him, but that I wanted to do it on my own, there's no way she wouldn't interfere. She couldn't help herself. She'd feel compelled to take it on, take it over. Then everyone else would get involved. My quest would become fodder for Friday night family conversation. It would become just like the Internet story. It would become just like Great Aunty Rita's jibes. This bit of the jigsaw that belonged to nobody but me would be reduced to another funny anecdote told by Aunt Lilah.

And that's why I had to do the searching myself. But how should I start? Maybe by making a list.

1. Name – I don't have one
2. Location – I don't know
3. Education – I have no idea

So far I'd tried Mum's handbags (thirteen in all) to see if she was keeping something back. I'd searched her dressing table and even under her bed. We didn't have a loft or a cupboard under the stairs, but if we had I'd have tried those too. So now what?

Even though I knew the Dadcard was probably not from Dad, since my birthday I just couldn't stop thinking about him and wondering what he would think of me if he could see me right now. So I did this thing that I used to do when I was a little kid where I pretended that my dad was looking over my shoulder and I was telling him stuff about what I did all day, like, '*Look – here's my bedroom. I chose this wallpaper when I was into Barbie, but now it just looks retarded, but Mum says we can't afford to change it right now.*' And, '*That's my ex-best-friend Shonna over there. Doesn't her hair look skanky to you?*'

So how the hell do you go about finding the person with whom you share your genetic heritage when you don't even know his name and you've already searched through your mum's thirteen handbags for clues and found zilch? It was time to enlist some help.

'DNA,' said Billy. 'We have his DNA, or rather *you* have his DNA.'

I was lying in the top bunk in Billy's room. He'd had these bunk beds since we were little kids. I used to be soooo jealous of them. I was lying there doing my usual thing of feeling around down the sides of the mattress, looking for those photos of Shonna from *The Wizard of Oz* that I knew were there somewhere. Billy went to see it three times. It was about then that Shonna told me Billy was 'getting kind of creepy'. Loads of girls would've been more than happy for my cousin to come watch them in some crappy school play three nights running, but Shonna was all, 'He's creeping me out, Sadie. I don't mean to be rude, but it's a bit freaky.'

When I think about stuff like that, I don't know why I ever liked Shonna Matthews.

Anyway, it felt like she wasn't in Billy's bunk any longer, that was for sure.

'Sadie, you won't find any dodgy mags up there,' said Billy, 'so you can stop digging around.'

'I'm not,' I lied, and pulled out a copy of *Guitar Now* featuring a Billy Zoom Custom Shop Tribute Silver Jet Gretsch as centrefold. Well dodgy.

'I can see your hands – get out of it. D'you want me to help you or what?'

'Yes,' I said because I really did want Billy Fact Man Superbrainbox to help me. 'OK, I don't even know where to start with all this.'

'Well, I've done a bit of research,' said Billy. 'There are websites.'

I popped my head down over the top bunk and stared at him upside down. 'Websites?' I said. 'You can do it on the Internet?'

'There are websites where you can send off your DNA to see if anyone in your dad's family has ever registered.'

'Really – people do that? Why would they?'

Billy lay back on his pillow and sighed through his nose. 'Genealogy, I suppose.' He shrugged. 'People want to trace their relations – maybe they think they might inherit something or other.'

'But how do I do it? How do I actually send off my DNA? Is it like a blood test? Because I really, really hate those.' The thought of it made me feel queasy.

'Getting your DNA is the easy bit,' said Billy snottily. Clearly he didn't care about my veins.

'Easy for you maybe – it's not your blood.' I was not entirely sure I could go through with this.

'Cheek swab. You just scrape your cheek and send it off.'

'Scrape?'

'On a cotton bud. They send you a kit, but essentially it's on a cotton bud.'

God, I love Billy. He is just so smart.

So we fired up Billy's laptop and we found the biggest site – familydna.com. But when we looked through the different tests, Billy started scratching his head and making a weird humming noise because they were all for men tracing their fathers.

'The trouble is,' said Billy, 'you don't have a Y chromosome.'

'So what does that mean?' I said. I had sort of guessed anyway – after all, I'd listened to some of Mr Graves's lessons on genetics, even though in general I spent double human biology staring at that spittle at the corners of his mouth, wondering whether his wife ever told him to wipe it away or if she'd just stopped noticing it. But I still wanted Billy to spell it out for me.

'DNA in the Y chromosome is passed from father to son – not from father to daughter, you see,' he told me. 'Boys have both the X and the Y, but girls only have the X. It means we can't trace your dad through one of these sites – it's not clever enough yet. You have your dad's X chromosome – actually, strictly speaking, you

58

have your dad's mother's X chromosome. But not the Y
– well, otherwise you'd be a bloke.'

I was starting to glaze over now. It was too much
information.

'So these tests,' Billy continued, 'they can't deal
with the X. They only deal with the Y and I'm afraid
you're sort of lacking in the Y chromosome department.'

I was lacking in the Dad department, the friend
department, and now I was lacking in the chromosome
department. I crawled back up to Billy's bunk and under
the duvet.

'I'm really sorry, Sadie,' said Billy.

He did sound sorry, but it was nice and snuggly
under the duvet and I really didn't want to come out. I
was all set to stay there for the rest of the day, but
Shonna Matthews drove me out eventually – or rather
the picture of her in her PE kit that I found in Billy's
pillowcase.

'Did you cut that out of the Yearbook, Billy?'

'Err yeah.'

'*That* is creepy.' I stuck my head back under the
pillow.

'Sadie,' I heard Billy say, 'maybe you should just talk

to your mum about your dad. Why don't you show her the stupid birthday card and just, y'know, ASK HER? She might not be able to tell you much, but she may know where to start looking.'

OK. Putting aside the bit about family interference, if I wanted to find out something about my Donor Dad then why the hell didn't I bite the bullet like Billy said? I should go home and ask Mum if she had any other details, instead of searching her handbags and fiddling around with cheek swabs.

But I couldn't just ask Mum.

I *couldn't*.

Could I?

9

No 1 is Listening

OK. So maybe Billy did have a point. Asking Mum would obviously be the most straightforward way of finding out stuff. Of course if I asked Mum then I would run the risk of her going into her speech about the Generosity of the Donors and how I was a Wanted Child, and her eyes would get misty and she'd probably call Aunt Lilah. But after all of that, maybe she would try and help. And like Billy said, she might not have all the information, but she could certainly help me find it. Maybe it *was* worth involving my family in order to spite the meangirlz and their stupid little joke. After all, my family were just really annoying – they weren't actually evil like Shonna and Imelda.

I'd more or less decided, by the time I put my key in the door of the flat, that I was going to broach the subject with Mum. And I was going to do it now. I wouldn't tell her about the Dadcard – cos she'd get all hung up on who sent it to me. So I'd just say that I was thinking about starting to look for the person who might be my genetic other half.

For some reason I felt weird about using the word Dad around Mum. After all, I wasn't really looking for an actual dad presence, was I? If I wanted a physical dad, I didn't need to look any further than Uncle Zé. He'd done a fine job of helping to bring me up – and we did have Aunt Lilah as well and she was more than enough relatives for anyone.

I could hear Mum on the phone as I opened the front door.

'I would like to speak to your manager, please.'

She was talking in her special SPEAKING TO AN IDIOT voice. It's pretty scary. I wouldn't like to be on the receiving end of those sort of calls – that's for sure.

'Are you telling me that there is no manager on the floor?'

Pause.

'So there's no manager on the floor?'

Pause.

'Well, I'd like to speak to him, please.'

Pause.

'If he's there, why does he have to ring me back?'

Pause.

'Are you telling me that there's no manager on the fl–'

Semi-pause.

'Please don't take that tone with me. I would like to remind you that I am the cust–'

Pause.

'You have put a stop on my account with no warning and I would like to speak to your . . . I WOULD LIKE TO SPEAK TO YOUR . . .'

There was another pause and then I heard a crash, which I took to be the sound of a phone being ripped out of the wall and hurled across a room. Instead of somebody's head. I peered round the door. Mum's eyes were red and her hair was fluffed up at the front from where she'd been running her fingers through it, which is what she does when she's on the phone to the bank or the credit card people, or anyone else who puts our bank accounts on 'stop', which they do sometimes when we're apparently least expecting it.

Mum does the bookkeeping for a lot of itty-bitty businesses in the area and she seems to get them to pay everybody's invoices on time except her own. For as long as I can remember, we have lurched from one financial crisis to another. This can be a little wearing on nerves and on phones. The point is that now didn't quite feel like the right moment to start asking Mum about the person who'd donated his sperm sixteen years ago.

But I really *did* want to ask her, now I'd worked up to it.

'Mum?' I said.

She was scrabbling in the corner, picking up pieces of broken phone and trying to fit them back together.

'Oh.' She looked round at me sheepishly. 'I dropped the phone a bit . . . well, actually, I threw the phone a bit.'

She held up two of the push-button numbers which had snapped off and started pointlessly trying to shove them back into the base unit.

'I think we may need a new one this time, Mum.' I said. 'I don't think you can just stick them on with jam or hammer them in with your shoe, y'know.'

'You're right.' She smiled at me and sank back on to the sofa surrounded by piles of papers.

My mum, she could be pretty, right? Bit of make-up, sort out the hair, some smart clothes on her neat little figure – she'd be this pint-sized executive type. The trouble is she has two hairstyles – both from about 1987 (which she will not let me sort), and both maintained by Aunt Lilah. Her make-up is generally au naturel, i.e. practically non-existent, and she wears colours that wash her out. When I look at her sometimes, I don't even feel related to her. Perhaps my dad has impeccable taste in hair and clothes. Well, there was only one way to find out. I took a deep breath.

'Are you all right?' interrupted Mum before I'd even started. 'You still look peaky, y'know.'

'I'm fine,' I said.

'You stay up too late,' said Mum. 'You stay up too late and you don't eat a proper breakfast. Oh my God, I never thought I would say stuff like *you stay up too late* and *you don't eat a proper breakfast* and *you never called* and *I was worried*!'

'I'm fine, really,' I said, ignoring Mum's rambling, which is something she always does. 'I'm not a three-year-old – you don't have to monitor my every move any more.'

'I'm your mother, it's what I do, and I don't monitor

your every move. You make me sound like I'm spying. I'm just concerned. I'm a concerned parent. It's my job.'

'Well then, it's my job to be a negative teenager.'

'I've never met anyone quite so well suited to their work.'

'Why don't you let me get on with it then?'

We were about to get into an argument. About nothing. I took another deep breath and tried again.

'Mum,' I said, 'can I talk to you about something quite important?'

She looked up at me almost as if she'd forgotten I was there.

'Huh? Look, sweetheart,' she said, putting her hand on my arm, 'if it's about the French trip, I think we're going to have to say no if they want the money now – I saw the note on the kitchen table. I'll make it up to you. We'll have a trip – maybe in the New Year.' Her eyes misted over.

The stoopid, dumb French trip. Where had *that* come from? Of course it wasn't about the French trip! In a former life I would have killed to have gone on that: Paris? Nice? The Loire? Shonna and me prancing down the Champs Elysées! But Shonna hates me and she's going with Imelda, so I'm kind of relieved that we can't afford it right now. It'd be twenty-four-hour torture.

'Actually, Mum,' I said, 'it isn't about the French trip.'

'Oh?' She looked up at me and took off her glasses. 'You know, you *do* look tired, pet. *I* am *so* tired.' She put her head back and closed her eyes. 'I've had such a helluva day. George from the record store is haemorrhaging money left, right and centre, and he wants me to perform some minor miracle on his books. I spent the whole day ringing suppliers trying to get an extension on his payments. I said to him, "George, love, you have to face up to the fact that no one is buying vinyl any more. It's all downloading and . . . God, you look bored, Sadie.'

'The thing is I was about to say something,' I said. 'Can you just let me finish?'

'Look, I'm *really* sorry about the French trip. I would like you to go more than anything, but –'

'It's not *about* the crappy French trip – I already said that!' I was angry now. 'Why don't you just listen to me?'

'There's no need to be so rude. I don't know what's wrong with you these days. You are *so* —'

And at that very moment the door buzzer went.

'I just wanted to talk to you,' I carried on over the insistent buzzer. I felt desperate and I had no idea how the conversation had ended up here. 'I didn't mean to be rude, but you weren't listening.'

'Well, I'm sorry,' said Mum, 'but I've had a helluva day.'

The door buzzer went again. Mum stood up.

'It's Tuesday,' she said. 'Of course — how could I forget?'

She went to the intercom.

Tuesday night meant only one thing in our house. *Good as it Gets* on the TV — starring Harry Hodder and playing live in our living room to a rapt audience of Mum and Aunt Lilah.

'Yoo-hoo!' I could hear Aunt Lilah shrieking into the intercom like we hadn't seen her for seven years or something — like she isn't round here the whole time or we're not over there every half hour. And now she was coming up the stairs, chocolates and wine in her arms ready for her favourite telly programme.

God, she was annoying sometimes. Most of the time actually.

'*Good as it Gets* semi-finals tonight! Thought I'd get us a treat!' she trilled, marching into the lounge and immediately taking ownership of it.

Don't get me wrong. Somewhere, somehow I do love my Aunt Lilah. She can be kind and she does usually mean well. But she manages to crowd you out of your own home and she also enjoys the most moronic television programmes known to man.

Take *Good as it Gets*, which features a parade of no-talents lumping about the stage singing out of tune, watched by a group of equally talentless judges – like Harry 'The Hurricane' Hodder, whose pointless catchphrase is, 'Be brave! Be brave!' I know Mum doesn't really like it, but for some reason Aunt Lilah hasn't taken the hint and insists on making an occasion out of it every time it's on TV.

I decided not to hang about. I'd got myself psyched to talk to Mum and now I had been completely blocked.

'I'm going to do my homework,' I announced.

I was sort of hoping Mum might discreetly try to find out what I'd been about to say to her. But no – she just came right out with it. In front of Aunt Lilah.

'Didn't you want to ask me something, love?'

'No,' I said. 'I have to do my homework.'

'Suspense too much for you?' said Aunt Lilah, 'Worried Brendan's not going to get through this week?'

'Not particularly,' I said, with as much disinterest as I could inject into two words.

'Suit yourself. Nice hair by the way, doll,' said Aunt Lilah.

In spite of how annoying she could be, I was really pleased Aunt Lilah had noticed my Prom Hair.

'It's from the calendar and it started out with more lift this morning, but it's kind of flattened out. I think the styling spray isn't strong enough.'

'Did you backcomb?'

'Yuh-huh!'

'Well, I don't know then. Too much straightening serum at the ends – could be weighing it down. But I like it,' she said. 'Very classy. Very sleek. One of my customers is getting married in a couple of weeks. I might try that out on her.'

Aunt Lilah helped herself to the remote and put the telly on full blast. I glanced over at Mum, still hoping she might get the hint and follow me.

'D'you want a chocolate?' she said.

'No,' I said abruptly and turned round. I did not want a chocolate.

'What I want is a conversation,' I said, but I said it out of earshot and to no one of course.

I wanted Mum to make some space for me so that I could ask her a difficult question. But apparently this was not possible. Or convenient. Or something. Clearly only George from Go Beats Vinyl! could command Mum's whole attention on demand. I got the raggedy bit that was left at the end of the day.

I was shutting the door to my bedroom when I heard Aunt Lilah say, 'Ooh dear, what's got into her?'

'Oh nothing,' said Mum. 'She is just so negative these days. Not enthusiastic any more. Just sarky comment after sarky comment. She told me fifteen was a terrible age last night. On her birthday!'

'Ha! She should try being fifty. That really blows,' said Aunt Lilah.

The injustice of these comments made me flinch. I was negative because Mum hadn't listened to me. I made up my mind then and there: Mum didn't deserve to be confided in or share my stuff. I'd needed her and she'd totally missed her cue. I could see now that I would have to do this thing alone after all — Y chromosome or no Y chromosome.

I plugged in my headphones and switched off the light so that there was just me, my music and Mum's laptop. All life outside my bedroom door had ceased. My world was now online. I hoped Groovechick2 would be there too.

Current Mood: Life sucks 2day

Groovechick2: Nodding guy?

SayD: Just nodding.

Groovechick2: Dad?

SayD: Searching

Groovechick2: Life sucks bcos?

SayD: No1 is listening

Groovechick2: I'm listening

SayD: Am confused

Groovechick2: Bout wot?

SayD: Everything. And I hate my mum

Groovechick2: Bit strong

SayD: Passionately dislike then

Groovechick2: She's all u got

SayD: I'm pissed off with her

Groovechick2: Tell her

SayD: She don't deserve to no

10

I'm Sure She's Hiding Something

Wednesday 26th September
Hairstyle: Angelina Half-up Half-down
This is an old-fashioned look given a modern twist *à la*
Angelina Jolie. To get this lift, backcomb the hair right
down to the roots. If you don't like to tease or backcomb
then how about a Bumpit? This is a fabulous insert that
will lift the hair and keep it half-up half-down all night long.

I am not going to school today was my first thought on
waking.

'I'm not going to school today,' I said to Mum.

She was standing by my bedroom door with her cup
of tea. I can't watch my Mum drink tea without wanting
to flick her. She always slurps it too fast and then makes
this terrible hiccuping sound. It's gross.

'Can I come in or are you going to throw something
at me?' she said.

'I wasn't the one who broke the phone,' I said, 'and anyway, Barbie's house is always open.'

Mum perched herself on the end of my bed. 'Are you ill or is this just a bad hair day?'

'Bit of both.'

The excitement of my birthday and the blank-page feeling had given way to a bit of a depression. I was still pissed off with Mum, plus my lip was hurting and I couldn't face Shonna and Imelda today. Really, I just wanted to be left alone.

'I've got a cracking headache. I really do think I'd better stay off school,' I lied.

Of course this was a really stupid thing to say because Mum automatically went into panic mode, like I had meningitis or a brain tumour or something. Don't forget that my family's default setting is hysteria.

'Oh my God! Can you put your chin on your chest?'

'Of course I can.'

'Well, do it then! Chin on chest now – for me.'

So I did and she calmed down.

'Listen, love,' she said, 'I'm really sorry about the French trip.'

Omigod. We were having that conversation again.

Never mind George's vinyl – we were a stuck record. She just didn't get it, did she?

'It's all right, Mum! I already said I didn't want to go!'

'OK, but I am sorry. You should be able to go on class trips. It's just difficult at certain times of the year. George hasn't paid me, Marianne hasn't paid me and Jeanette swears she put the money into my account last week – but I'll be buggered if I've seen a penny of it.'

Then she recounted the conversation I'd half overheard with the bank the day before.

'I tell you – I know being fifteen isn't as carefree as I remember it but really you wouldn't want to swap your day for mine.'

'Well, I wouldn't want to swap your hair for mine, that's for sure.'

'Cheeky.'

'Why won't you let me have a go at your hair, Mum? You saw what I did with Billy's.'

'Your Aunt Lilah has always done my hair. She'd kill me. Seriously.'

Mum left for work and made me promise that I'd call her should any weird symptoms appear, like strange rashes or blinding flashes of light. Once she was safely out of the flat and I had the place to myself, I tried out the Angelina Half-up Half-down look. I didn't have a Bumpit, but I knew Mum had an ornamental comb somewhere that would probably do the trick in terms of lift.

Searching for the comb led to some good old-fashioned foraging in her stuff, like I've done a million times. When I was a little kid I used to pull out all her boxes of tampons and old packets of pills and treasured pictures of her mother – my nan – from her chest of drawers. Wedged behind her dressing table there was an ancient, enormous PC and on top of this was Mum's Special Box, where she keeps my birth certificate and the red book that has a record of all my jabs in it and how much I weighed when I was born. Why hadn't I thought of checking that before?

I flicked through it. Seems like I was in the bottom percentile for weight and height from the word go. According to the book, I had infantile eczema and even at one point 'Unequal buttock size and leg length'. Good God – as if things weren't bad enough: no friends and now a wonky bum.

I stood in front of Mum's full-length mirror for half

a minute, trying to check if my cheeks were still odd sizes. Leafing through to the end of the book, I found comments about my being an 'active, talkative child. No problems reported' and I felt much better. But there was nothing of any interest about my dad. There never was. According to Mum, that's because nothing existed. She had told me everything she knew. Apparently.

I lay back on Mum's pillows pretending that this was my room, and imagining where I would hide stuff if it was. I glanced up at the black-and-white photo Mum keeps on her bedside table. It's a picture of me as a baby. I have one totally perfect tooth (not a chip in sight) and I'm smiling up at the camera in this really unselfconscious, uncomplicated way, like, 'Hey look at my cool tooth!'

When did life start to get complicated? Was it when I got my second tooth?

When do kids get their teeth? Aged one or two? I picked up the photo frame and turned it round to see if there was a date on it. Pencilled in the corner was a number, partially obscured by the catch that held the picture in the frame. I slid the catch back and then I saw something else. A yellow piece of paper wedged in behind the cardboard backing and the photo. I took a sharp breath in. What the hell was this?

Carefully I pressed the cardboard forwards, slipped my fingers in and slid the paper out. This could be what I was looking for. Something about my dad. A vital piece of the puzzle that would tell me a detail – a name perhaps. I unfolded it, almost tearing it in my desperation to see what it was.

It turned out to be a birthday card from Great Aunty Rita sent fourteen years ago. It had a picture of some spring lambs gambolling about on the front and inside it said *Happy 1st Birthday Sadie From Great Aunty Rita*. Just like the one she sent this year of course. Same picture. Same message. What a total let-down.

I picked up Mum's Special Box and sat down on the ancient computer. I wondered if there were any hidden compartments I'd missed. Any false linings. But there was nothing.

I texted Billy. He would be on a home-study period.

SD: I'm sure she's hiding sthing. I can feel it

Billy: Yes probably – did u ask her for help?

SD: No

Billy: Y not?

My phone rang. It was Billy. Home-study period must be boring him.

'I checked the whole flat,' I said.

'Laptop?'

'I've checked that before.'

'Suitcase under the bed? My mum keeps everything there. She's even got my baby teeth and hair and stuff.'

'*Yeuch*. She's got a Special Box. I've checked that. I did find my first birthday card from Aunty Rita though and guess what?'

'What?'

'It was exactly the same one I got the other day.'

'The lambs?'

'Same.'

'So how come you get the lambs and I get the tractors?'

'She must have bought two multipacks sixteen years ago.'

'Should run out by the time we're twenty maybe.'

80

'If we're lucky. I just can't think of anywhere else to look.'

'Old computer? Does she have an old computer – like an ancient one that she had before the laptop?'

I looked down. Of course she did. I was sitting on it.

'Yeah, but this thing is a dinosaur and it's huge.'

Seemed unlikely, but I guessed the computer might be worth looking at. If you could get into it. Billy was pretty smart. And I did know that Tony Cruz was extremely handy with computers too.

'Bring it on over,' said Billy.

'The only thing is,' I said, 'it's so enormous and heavy and I don't know how I'll get it there.'

'Well, you figure that out,' said Billy, 'and I'll get on to Tony. If anyone can get into that dinosaur he can. He's like a Linux guru. I'll give him the GA.'

Billy was whirring and bleeping at me like he was in supernerd overdrive.

'You'll give him the what?'

'The GA. The Go Ahead.'

Haircut aside, Billy was such a dork.

*

I pulled on some tracksuit bottoms and a polo neck and my brand new Uggs (after all if there was the slightest chance I might run into Tony Cruz then I wanted to look OK). You know what? I looked good. Shonna used to get jealous over my ability to get dressed and look decent with apparently minimal effort.

'It takes me four hours to get ready and you zip around for ten minutes and you look better than me. Maybe it's because you're a shrimp. You have a smaller surface area to cover with clothes and make-up,' she'd say. It made me sad to think about Shonna being nice to me. I wanted to call her up and tell her I missed her so much that it was almost like a pain sometimes.

But if I did, she'd just laugh at me. I buried the thought and concentrated on trying out a hairstyle which would lift at the roots without backcombing.

I found Mum's ornamental comb in the bathroom cabinet and put it in my hair according to the instructions in my calendar, brushing my hair forward and securing it in a ponytail. As promised, it gave both lift and volume.

Then I looked around for something to load the enormous PC into that could be wheeled. All of our suitcases seemed to have wheels missing or broken zips, and the only thing left was one of Great Aunty Rita's old-lady walker/trolley things. You know, the ones elderly people put their shopping in, but also ram into you on the bus so you get out the way? Well, it was one of those. Nice red tartan one with a criss-cross metal chassis. I put an old sheet over the top as a cover and lugged it out the front door.

I managed to get it down in the lift and then I had to think of a reason I was wheeling it and I had to think of it fast because I could see the 50p lady coming towards me and I knew she'd ask.

'Spare 50p, love?' she said.

'Sorry, no,' I said.

'What's in there?' She eyed Aunty Rita's trolley.

'Laundry,' I said. I watched her expression to see if she thought it odd at all.

'Oh,' she said, 'laundry,' and walked on.

It takes less than five minutes to get from my place to Billy's. You just have to go down to the end of my road, past the minimarket, over the crossing and straight on by the cab firm, the posh cake shop, the Kebab-Tech, Ken's newsagent's and finally you got to Aunty&Uncle

Central: Café Zé and Deliah's salon. I've lived in this area my whole life and so every shop threatened a potential nosy parker about to ask me what was in my trolley.

'What's in the trolley, dear?' said Rez, one of the cab-drivers.

'Laundry.'

'Aha.'

'Where you off to with that trolley?' said Ken. 'You been doing your aunty's shopping, you good girl?'

'Laundry.'

'Oho.'

I passed Uncle Zé's café. He frowned at the trolley, but he was serving customers so he wasn't able to come running out to ask me about what was in it. Now I just had to wheel it through Aunt Lilah's salon and I was practically home and dry. There was a familiar smell of burnt hair and sickly, scented vanilla candles in Aunt Lilah's shop. I nodded a 'hello' to Aunt Lilah's back as she attacked some poor victim with the straightening irons.

'Where you going?' she called after me. 'Why aren't you in—'

'I'm not well!' I called back.

I could hear her tutting. 'Not well! We could all breeze about when we're not well – although' (she was talking to her customer now) 'she did pass out the other night. Right into her dinner.'

I could hear Aunt Lilah as I struggled up the stairs to their flat, still lugging the trolley and bashing their wallpaper on the way. 'Pork belly and rice – yeah, really nice the way he does it. It's the fish sauce.' Her voice faded away as I reached the top of the stairs and made my way to Billy's bedroom.

Billy and Tony were waiting for me. My heart turned over in my chest. Billy was doing his weird humming thing again and Tony was all blue-eyed and keenly nodding with his little kit of special computer tools.

Tony Cruz was undeniably hot, but really he and Billy were just a right couple of geeks.

11

Mumworld

'Wow!' said Billy. 'This thing really is out of the ark.'

We stared at the computer plonked in the middle of Billy's bedroom floor. We'd basically had to rearrange his entire bedroom to accommodate it.

'Should be in a museum,' said Tony.

They plugged it in, connected it to a screen and Tony fired it up. We watched it flicker into life. It made a groaning sound like someone was winding it up. The screen went blank and the orange cursor flickered on the left hand side.

'We need a password,' said Tony, standing up.

'Easy,' I said, '2409SN. My birthday. My initials.'

'This PC is pre-you,' said Billy, 'so unless Aunt Angela was psychic, it won't be your birthday.'

Duh. I looked at Tony to see if he thought I was an idiot. He didn't look like he was thinking anything. In fact, his head wasn't even nodding for once. He was doing this thing where he leans against the wall and closes his eyes. It's totally cool and makes him look really deep, unlike the nodding thing.

'No idea of the password,' I said. 'Does that mean we can't get in?'

I prepared myself for one giant let-down, but my question seemed to spur Tony into action. He opened his eyes and began one of those whirring and bleeping conversations with Billy. As nothing they said made any sense to me, I climbed up to Billy's bunk and put my head under the pillow, clenching my fists hard. The suspense was practically killing me.

'Sadie, you can come out,' said Billy eventually.

'Is it all over? We can't get in, right?'

'Nope, we *can* get in,' said Billy calmly. 'This is why God gave us Tony.' He smiled.

'Actually,' said Tony, 'this is why God gave us Linux.' He winked at me. For a computer nerd he is cute. My hands went to my hair. The comb was still in place giving both lift and volume. I couldn't check myself in the mirror though because Billy doesn't have one. (How can a nearly-sixteen-year-old boy not have a mirror? It's inhuman, I'm telling you.)

Tony put a CD in the computer drive and rebooted.

The search was still on. I climbed out of the bunk stiffly. All my muscles had tensed. I could feel my stubby nails sticking into my palms where I was clenching my fists. We were potentially about to unlock something major here.

Tony did what looked like a few simple keystrokes. I peered over at him. His long fingers were precise, like he was performing a delicate operation. Then he ejected the CD and sat back.

'OK,' he said, 'password no longer needed.'

'Well done,' I said. He was a complete genius.

'Number one geek, my man!' said Billy, and he and Tony high-fived one another.

Why do boys do that? If they only knew that it kills any cuteness.

Tony and Billy swapped places now and Billy rebooted, leaving the prompt for password blank.

We were in Mum's PC and we were entering virtual Mumworld – the world before and just after she had me. There were emails going back seventeen years on the ancient thing and it carried on creaking and groaning with the sheer effort of having to display them all after so long.

'OK,' said Billy, 'how long does it take to make a baby? Nine months – so let's go back to the September a year before you were born.'

He scrolled down the list of senders. 'GColes@ babymakers maybe?'

It was one email – an automated response to say that G Coles was on holiday, but would answer the query on his/her return. The sign-off was 'Happy Babymaking!' which seemed a bit flippant for a website accessed by people desperate to have children. No wonder there was only one email – that response was enough to put you off contacting them again.

'OK, enqs@fertility-in-touch.com maybe?' said Billy.

It sounded plausible. It sounded promising. We peered over his shoulder.

There were a lot of admin-type emails from that address – 'thank you for your enquiry' and so forth, and lots of information on how the service worked. It turned out that this website was like a posting box between donors and mothers. The website kept the details of the dads for the mothers to look through, and then contacted the donors if they were 'chosen' and once everything was agreed they arranged a courier service for the 'donation'. It was a disclosure programme and so all the donors had to agree to register their contact details as well as full medical and family histories.

'Wow,' said Tony. 'Lot of paperwork here.'

Then finally we came upon something substantial.

From: enqs@fertility-in-touch.com

Sent: Wed 28th Sept 11.26

To: a.nathanson@parksidebookkeeping.co.uk

Subject: donors 241, 254, 278

Dear Ms Nathanson

Thank you for your enquiry and finder's fee.

I am pleased to enclose the details of selected donors (attached).

Donor 241, 254, 278

Regards

Lucy Botham

Enquiries Administrator

Donors. Donors were mentioned. Donors and numbers. A shiver went down my spine. OK. This was actually happening now. We were finding something out here. But where was the attachment with the details of the donors?

Billy scrolled up and down the email. His eyes flicked around the screen, searching.

'There's no attachment,' he said eventually.

'Of course there's no attachment,' I said, because I knew that it couldn't be that easy. It wasn't like there was going to be a PDF attached with an address, phone number, Winston-Churchill-Baby photo and 'worry crinkle' listed as a distinguishing mark on it.

There was, however, one other email from Lucy Botham, Enquiries Administrator.

From: enqs@fertility-in-touch.com
Sent: Wed 24th Oct 09.31
To: a.nathanson@parksidebookkeeping.co.uk
Subject: re. thank you
Dear Ms Nathanson
Thank you for your email and congratulations on the birth of your baby girl.
We are always delighted to receive news of births of clients or former clients at fertility-in-touch.com.
Best wishes to you and your family.

I looked at the date on the email: 24th October. I would have been one month old.

'Woah,' said Tony. His head was bobbing up and down. 'This is significant.'

'This is it!' said Billy.

But it wasn't 'it' yet, although my heart, which was beating at twice its usual speed, seemed to think that this actually was 'it'.

'This is what?' I said. I wanted someone to say it out loud.

'This email is confirmation. The website. This is where Aunty Angela got the donor – your dad,' said Billy. 'Fertility-in-touch.com.'

He was right. They were both right. I exhaled very slowly, like I'd been holding my breath for the longest time. I was too stunned to say anything. I just clenched and unclenched my fists. Then I leaned over Billy and scrolled down the email to the original one that Mum had sent, the email that Lucy whatsername was replying to. Mum's email was sent at 2.26 in the morning. I guess I wasn't much of a sleeper in those days. I tried to imagine Mum sitting in the half-light of our flat typing that email, staring out over the houses while I gurgled about on the rug.

Her own message said simply:

From: a.nathanson@parksidebookkeeping.co.uk
Sent: Wed 24th Oct 02.26
To: enqs@fertility-in-touch.com
Subject: thank you
Dear Lucy
This is just to let you know that my daughter, Sadie, was born on 24th September. I wanted to thank you for your help and interest in making this happen.
With many thanks
Angela Nathanson

I wondered if she'd had any regrets at the time she wrote that email, about what she'd done, about having me. I'm fairly sure she does now.

'She doesn't say *which* donor she used,' said Tony.

'Which one was it, Aunty Angela?' said Billy to the

computer. '241, 254 or 278 . . . come on!'

The boys were staying focused on the trail while I'd wandered off on a tangent about my sleeping habits.

'Do a search for the attachment,' said Tony.

Billy checked the C: drive and, sure enough, among the folders of Excel spreadsheets belonging to Mum's clients was one with the likely title of 'Project Baby'. Mumworld was so obvious!

But the Project Baby folder was empty.

I stared hard at the screen, willing it to deliver up something tangible. Billy did a search for '241' then '254' and then '278', but nothing came up.

I was sweating now. My forehead felt moist, as if my freshly applied make-up was sliding down my cheeks. If only there was a mirror.

'Just try all the folders,' said Tony. 'See if any of them are passworded.'

For twenty minutes Billy painstakingly clicked on and off the folders on the C: drive, while it whirred and groaned like it was about to take off.

'This one,' he said eventually. 'No title and it's password protected.'

I breathed in. 'OK. Now what?' I said.

'We need to run the password reveal tool,' said Billy.

Of course we did and of course Tony Cruz reached into his pocket and took out the USB stick which he carried with him and that held the password reveal tool. He sat down again, plugged in the stick and performed the delicate keystrokes while I paced the bedroom.

Wasn't this what men did in old movies while their wives were having babies? They paced while other people did stuff: the doctors, the nurses, the wives. It was weird. I was pacing the room to find out who would have paced the room if this had been an old movie, if you see what I mean. If this was an old movie and I was a man, I would have had a buzz cut. I wondered whether I could do a buzz cut. You needed clippers. Maybe I should get a Saturday job at the E9 Barber to learn how to handle clippers. I was pretty sure Aunt Lilah couldn't manage a buzz cut . . .

'We're in,' said Tony suddenly.

I took in a sharp gulp of air. This could not be happening. It simply could not be that easy. Surely not. Surely not.

And then he said, 'I think this is what we're looking for.'

I felt a small dribble of sweat launch itself from my armpit and ooze slowly and coolly down the inside of my arm. My heart felt as if it was leaping out of my chest.

I peered at the screen. There were three separate documents. Three documents. Three donors but no clue as to which one was actually my dad.

241

254

278

We just stared silently at the files while Tony hovered the mouse over each one in turn, not knowing which to open.

'For God's sake!' said Billy eventually. 'Which one is it?'

'It's all three,' said Tony. 'What d'you think, Sadie? Should we open all three?'

'I guess,' I said quietly. 'I mean, why not?'

There was a noise from outside the door and we all jumped. Uncle Zé was coming upstairs, calling down to Aunt Lilah in the shop.

'Getting a Coke!' he was shouting. 'Want one?'

And then he was outside Billy's door, knocking.

I didn't want Uncle Zé to come into the room. I

didn't want him to see that we had a great big old PC in here. He'd want to know what it was, what we were doing. He'd ask questions. He'd get suspicious.

So I ran to the door and opened it a crack. I felt like there was a tiny bird caught in my chest, my heart was thumping and fluttering so wildly. I could hear the boys scrambling around in the background trying to hide Mum's computer.

'Hi, *tito*,' I said, smiling broadly and sounding ever so chatty. 'Really sorry about the other night – the ruining your lovely dinner bit.'

'S' OK, *anak*, we'll do it again sometime,' said Uncle. He was trying to look past me into the bedroom, but I shut the door behind me and steered him towards the kitchen.

'I'd love a Coke,' I said. 'I'm sure Billy would too.'

I heard Billy's printer whirring into action from the bedroom.

'And Tony?' said Uncle Zé, staring meaningfully at me, 'What do you think that Tony would like?'

'I . . . I don't know what Tony would like. A Coke I guess.' I was feeling guilty . . . about having recently stood in the same room as Tony Cruz.

'You think Tony's OK?' said Uncle Zé casually as he poured the drinks. 'Do you like him, *anak*?'

This was a trick question, right?

'Tony's just . . . well, he's just Tony.'

'And you like him?' insisted Uncle.

'Sure I like him – he seems really . . .'

'Nice? Kind? Cute?'

Uncle was setting a trap. I knew it was a trap.

'Sure, he's NICE,' I said very firmly so that there could be no room for doubt. Uncle Zé needed to lighten up about boys. In some ways life would have been so much easier if Uncle Zé was my actual dad because that's how he behaved – it's like he owned me.

'Wanna Coke, Billy *iho*?' said Uncle Zé, and there stood Billy and Tony in the kitchen doorway – a little flushed, but cool as cucumbers really.

'Yeah, two, please,' said Billy. He mouthed '*in the bedroom*' at me and then entered the kitchen.

I retreated to Billy's bedroom where they had managed to hook up a printer which was randomly spitting out papers into a heap on the floor.

I gathered them up and began to sort them into order.

Charles Ward	
charles.ward2@hotmail.com	Donor: 254
Marital Status:	Single
Number of Children:	0
Religion:	Christian
Occupation:	Actor
Blood Type:	O+
Ethnicity:	English
Medication Allergy:	No
Food Allergy:	No
Pet Allergy:	No
Hay Fever Allergy:	Yes
Insect Allergy:	No
Vaccine Allergy:	No
Healthy Teeth:	Yes
Braces:	Yes
Back Problems:	No
Bronchitis:	No
Chicken Pox:	Yes
Chicken Pox Age:	2
Vertigo:	No
Mental Health:	Good

Richard Swain-Coles	
r.swaincoles@doctorsnet.org.uk	Donor: 278
Marital Status:	Single
Number of Children:	0
Religion:	Agnostic
Occupation:	Medical Student
Blood Type:	O +
Ethnicity:	English
Medication Allergy:	No
Food Allergy:	No
Pet Allergy:	No
Hay Fever Allergy:	No
Insect Allergy:	No
Vaccine Allergy:	No
Healthy Teeth:	Yes
Braces:	No
Back Problems:	No
Bronchitis:	No
Chicken Pox:	Yes
Chicken Pox Age:	5
Vertigo:	No
Mental Health:	Good

Abraham Smith	
abe.smith@kent.gov.uk	Donor: 241
Marital Status:	Single
Number of Children:	0
Religion:	Agnostic
Occupation:	Municipal Gardener
Blood Type:	O+
Ethnicity:	English
Medication Allergy:	No
Food Allergy:	No
Pet Allergy:	No
Hay Fever Allergy:	No
Insect Allergy:	No
Vaccine Allergy:	No
Healthy Teeth:	Yes
Braces:	No
Back Problems:	No
Bronchitis:	No
Chicken Pox:	Yes
Chicken Pox Age:	3
Vertigo:	Yes
Mental Health:	Good

Charles Ward. Richard Swain-Coles. Abraham Smith.

Actor. Doctor. Gardener.

This was it then. The donor numbers had become names and occupations. These were my dads' details.

All three of them.

Because, even looking at the details, there was no indication at all as to which one was really mine.

12

If Your Dad Was a Sperm Donor

After a while, Billy came back into the bedroom, sat down at the computer and began doing his weird humming thing while I stared and stared at the printouts. I was having trouble taking it all in. What we'd just found out was more information than I'd had before. The trouble was, it was more information than I really needed. If there had just been one printout . . .

I stared out of the window blankly. The Royal Standard Tandoori sign opposite was winking incessantly, as it always had. Mr Khan was looking out of its front window, glumly surveying the street for early customers. He looked up and smiled at me and half waved. I nodded. I knew Mr Khan a lot better than I knew Richard Swain-Coles, Abraham Smith or Charles Ward, even though I shared genes with one of them. I knew Ken the newsagent, the 50p lady and Colin from the Vietnamese on the corner a lot better than I knew my dad.

'What do you think then?' said Billy eventually. 'Me and Tony — we reckon you should email them. Ask if they're your dad.'

I didn't say anything. The situation was too twisted for colour TV.

'Well, that's what I would do,' said Billy.

'Oh,' I said, 'so that's what you would do if your dad was a sperm donor and you had a choice of three that you'd just hacked off your mum's computer? And anyway, chances are they won't even know if they are my dad. I'm sure Mum didn't call them up to congratulate them on the quality of their contribution.'

'I just—' said Billy.

'No! That's fine,' I said. 'That's good to know what *you* would do.'

I carried on staring rigidly out of the window. I didn't want to be having this conversation. It was stoopid. Who would know what to do in this situation? *No one* was ever in this situation. Except me of course.

'Sorry,' said Billy. 'I didn't mean—'

'I'm just feeling a bit weirded out right now,' I said, 'and you telling me what you and Tony would do doesn't really help me, because it's not you, it's me.'

'Sorry,' said Billy again.

'I mean, whoever heard of IVF resulting in multiple Dads?'

Billy laughed and then tried to cover it up with a cough when he saw my face, which was giving him the evils.

'I need to take it all in and absorb it before I go any further,' I said. 'I have names now – which is kind of a bigger deal than I realised.'

Billy looked a bit disappointed. Out of the corner of my eye I saw his shoulders slump.

'I don't want to stop looking,' I said, 'but I think I need some air and some space before I do anything else. And I've got to get the computer back home before Mum notices it's gone.'

'Sure,' said Billy.

With Tony's help, we loaded the PC back into the old-lady trolley and lifted it down the stairs as quietly as possible. Not quietly enough because Uncle Zé poked his head out of the lounge and watched us.

'Laundry,' I said.

Either I spoke convincingly or Uncle Zé was distracted by the fact that Tony Cruz was standing less than a metre away from me when I said it. Whatever, he seemed satisfied with this explanation and went back into the lounge without questioning me further, but with a grumpy look on his face.

Aunt Lilah had a client in the shop who she was busily wrapping in tinfoil like a giant turkey. She didn't even turn round as I breezed through.

I wheeled the PC back down the street and it was a relief to see that everything was just the same. Nothing had changed in my neighbourhood even if everything felt like it had changed in my head. I breathed out and my pulse slowed.

As I turned into my road, I could see the kitchen light on from the street. Dammit, Mum was in, which meant I'd have to somehow sneak the PC back into her bedroom without her clocking it.

For no particular reason I picked up a chalky stone and drew a love heart on the red-brick wall outside the flats. In the middle I wrote RSC and AS and CW. The initials of all the dads from the printouts.

'How funny,' I imagined myself saying casually to Shonna in a parallel life where we were still mates and walking to school with our arms linked, 'those are my dads' initials.'

'You're so lucky,' Shonna would say. 'You have three dads and all your dads are so coooool.'

'Those are your dads' initials,' Mum would say in that alternate world. 'They'll find that hilarious. We must point it out to them when they get home from work.'

But none of these things will ever happen because Shonna Matthews hates me, Mum won't listen to me, and RSC, AS and CW don't even know they have a fifteen-year-old daughter living in Hackney, East London.

13

Whateva, Mum

Before I'd even got into the flat I could hear Great Aunty Rita's voice vibrating through the front door. As always, she sounded like she was speaking through a loudhailer. This was good news as it meant that Mum wouldn't hear me as she'd be pinned into her seat trying not to flinch.

I crept into the hall, put the trolley back in its place and heaved the PC out. I carried it back into Mum's bedroom on tiptoe and wedged it behind the dressing table with her Special Box on the top. Then I took a deep breath and opened the door to the living room.

Mum and Great Aunty Rita were sitting at the table eating pickled cucumbers. *Eww*. They both looked surprised to see me.

'Aha,' boomed Great Aunty Rita, 'my favourite great-niece.'

Then she cracked up and I pretended to as well,

even though it was the bazillionth time I'd heard it.

'Hi, Aunty Rita,' I said. I gave her a big hug. She is a scary old lady, but I do sort of love her as well. She's my surrogate grandparent and I think she does pretty well, although Mum says she interferes too much.

I don't have real grandparents — they died within three years of one another when Mum and Aunt Lilah were still in primary. We don't talk about them too much because it makes everyone so sad — I mean, I even start to feel sorry for Aunt Lilah when I think about it. Mum and Aunt Lilah and Great Aunty Rita go to synagogue once a year and pray for my grandparents and listen to Kol Nidrei, which is like this incredibly sad song all in a minor key which makes you feel practically suicidal.

Sometimes Mum'll get the photos out to check if I'm looking like her mother yet, but it's very hard to tell from the pictures because they're so over-coloured or faded and grainy. Whenever I complain too much that our family live in each other's pockets, Mum will remind me of how lucky I am that we all have one another. Lately it's been real hard to view this as 'lucky'. Like now for instance.

'You've been out?' said Mum after I'd hugged Aunty

Rita. 'My God, you look pale and hot.' She grabbed my hand. 'And your palms are clammy. I think you've got a temperature. Rita, she's got a temperature.'

No wonder I was pale and hot and clammy – I'd just discovered I had three potential dads and I'd been lugging a five kilo PC around – on tiptoe.

'She's fine, Angela,' said Aunty Rita. 'Really, it's a lot of fuss. D'you want a pickled cucumber, dear? These are good. They have dill.'

'No thanks, Aunty.' I have never been a pickle fan.

'Angela she doesn't want a pickle!' said Aunty Rita. 'She's sick.'

I *hate* pickles.

'She's never eaten pickles,' said Mum.

'Never eaten pickles?' said Aunty Rita. 'There's something wrong, I'm telling you, Angela. You're not well, Sadie. Sit down, get your breath.'

'I'm OK really,' I said. 'I just needed some air. I went out for a walk.'

Aunty Rita watched me as I sat down at the table. Then she handed me a pickle. I ate it simply because I couldn't be bothered to have the pickle conversation again. That's what they're like – old people – they wear you down and then you find yourself eating a gherkin against your will.

'Still enjoying school?' asked Aunty Rita.

This was like asking whether I enjoyed being in a daily car crash.

'Sure,' I said.

'And how is Gad?' she said.

For a split second I couldn't quite remember who Gad was. And then I thought *Dad, Gad,* and the whole thing with the birthday card and Billy leaping in to help all came back.

'Oh, he's OK, Aunty Rita,' I managed, almost without missing a beat.

'I've never even heard of Gad,' Mum sniffed. She raised her eyebrows at me and then looked away. 'But I suppose I'd be the last to hear these days.'

This is sort of true I guess, but I'm not entirely sure why Mum has to say it. It's like it's supposed to be funny or something, but it isn't funny at all because no one's laughing so it just ends up being annoying and sarcastic. And of course I decided to challenge her.

'What d'you mean, you'd be the last to know?' I said. 'Weren't you there on my birthday when I got that card from Gad?' I didn't wait for her answer. 'I mean, everyone else can remember it – so why can't you?'

I could feel the colour rising in my face. After all, this was all her fault; if she'd just listened to me the other day when I needed to talk to her, I wouldn't be doing this whole Dad-thing on my own.

I turned abruptly and marched to the kitchen area. I picked up a large knife and plunged it into a block of cheese sitting on the worktop. It was a surprisingly satisfying manoeuvre.

'I saw Jeanette today at the shop,' said Mum.

And she stared round at me, meaningfully. I continued hacking at the cheddar.

Let me explain: Shonna Matthews's mum, Jeanette, runs a dress shop called Empire of Bling down the Roman Road. It's all leopard print and lime-green thongs and my mum is her bookkeeper. Jeanette Matthews and Mum aren't exactly close friends any more, not since Shonna and me were little kids, but they still like to gossip. Maybe Mum had found out about Shonna and Imelda being best friends now. Maybe she'd heard about the chipped tooth – and all from Shonna's point of view. I said nothing. There was not a lot to say.

'Honey, did you hear me?' Mum carried on. 'I said I saw Jeanette.'

'I heard you, Mum,' I said. I was trying to screen her out. Now I was concentrating on slicing the cheese as thinly as possible without damaging my thumb.

'Honey, she was . . . honey, can you come over here and sit down?'

'Talk to your mother, dear!' bellowed Aunty Rita through her loudhailer.

I had managed to slice the cheese really thin and then I picked up the nail scissors that were in the kitchen drawer and started to clip away at the cheese like it was hair. I was thinking, *I know I'd be great with clippers — maybe I will go and see the E9 Barber about that job so I can learn how to do a buzz cut . . .*

'Sadie!' Mum raised her voice.

'Come and sit down!' boomed Aunty Rita, and then, 'Dear,' she said quietly as an afterthought.

It was bad enough dealing with Shonna at school without having to talk about her at home. Mum looked a bit hurt, as if having to raise her voice a little above a murmur was really quite distressing. She held out her hand to me and gestured towards the other chair.

'Sweetheart, why didn't you tell me you and Shonna still aren't speaking?'

Typically she didn't really give me time to answer, but carried straight on.

'Jeanette says she can't understand what's been going on between the two of you, but she says Shonna's really upset about it.'

Yeah right, I thought. *Which bit is she upset about? The bit where I didn't hit the floor hard enough to crack my skull?* Maybe I should have told Mum. Maybe I should've said, 'Mum, the truth is that Shonna has made my life a living hell ever since she told everyone my dad was sperm chosen off the Internet. She follows me around. She bullies me. She even sent me a fake birthday card and signed it "Dad". I hate her.'

But I didn't say that. Why would I? So Angela could ring Jeanette? So that the two Mummys who'd spent all those years arranging sleepovers and playdates and outings, and who'd got to know one another's daughters like they were their own, could get us in a room to 'talk about it'? Shonna would just use it all as more ammunition for humiliating me in school. I didn't trust her.

'We've grown apart, Mum,' I said. 'It can happen you know.'

'I know, darling. I just think it must make you miserable – you used to do everything together.'

She was right. I knew everything about Shonna Matthews that there was to know. I knew that the bracelet on her left wrist was the christening one she'd had since birth, that she moved it along a notch every year. I knew that the spare key to her flat was under a stone tortoise in her nan's front garden next door. I knew that Shonna had a strawberry birthmark on her leg which we called 'the creeping rosemary', which started at her ankle and went all the way up her thigh. I knew that if someone farted, Shonna would ask, 'Who's fluffed a pinkie?' That always cracked me up.

'You two were the greatest friends,' said Mum.

'Well, I was great friends with Rabbi Rabbit once, but we grew apart too.'

Which is a good point actually. Rabbi Rabbit was my number one bedtime friend who I went through thick and thin with as a kid. She sits on a shelf now with her stuffing trailing out of a tear in her arm.

'I'm just saying,' Mum droned on pointlessly. 'I'm just saying.'

She looked tired. Her minimal make-up has generally slid off her face by the end of the day and her features look washed out. Plus, on this particular evening, her baggy sweater had a stain on the arm, and her hair – OMG! Bad hair is all I'm saying. I *never* want to look like that when I'm forty-eight.

I stood up. 'Shonna's changed,' I said. 'I prefer hanging out with Billy these days.'

'With Billy or with Tony?' said Mum.

Mum's seen Tony. She knows he's hot.

'Yes, Tony is Billy's mate, but I don't–' I started.

'And who,' bellowed Great Aunty Rita like an old foghorn, 'is Tony? I thought the boy's name was Gad.'

'Like I said,' said Mum, 'I'd be the last to know who Gad is. But Jeanette did mention Tony.' She looked at me. 'She said it's Tony who's come between you and Shonna. She says Shonna likes Tony, but she can't get near because you're always hanging around him.'

That did it. How dare she! Hanging around?

'Jeanette Matthews,' my voice was loud – as loud as Aunty Rita's now, 'can go to hell! I am not *hanging around*!

I don't have any other friends and I need somewhere to go.' I wiped the stupid tears away and made a run for it. I didn't want Mum to know my damage. It was like giving in. I wanted to be on my own with it. I grabbed the laptop on my way out. Bedroom door slammed and locked this time. Headphones jammed over my ears muffling Mum's insistent knocking.

'Sadie, love, let's talk about it. There's obviously a lot going on right now.'

Later I heard Aunty Rita getting ready to leave. She and Mum were stood in the hallway for a while.

'I hate to butt in,' said Aunty Rita. 'Of course you know what you're doing, Angela, but I do think if you'd have sent her to the Hillel Heights school for Jewish girls then you wouldn't be having this problem.'

'Rita, if she was at Hillel Heights then she'd be having all kinds of other problems fitting in – like: *What d'you mean I can't eat pork?* I'd rather she falls out with her best friend over a boy – it's far less complicated.'

I heard Mum let Great Aunty Rita out and she must have stood in the hall a really long time. Later still I heard her calling Aunt Lilah.

'I just don't know what's the matter!' was all I heard her say before she shut the lounge door.

My room was dark now. I stood up and pulled Rabbi Rabbit down from her dusty shelf and put her in bed next to me. She still smelled exactly like she used to.

I unfolded Mum's laptop. On the net Groovechick2's **Current Mood** was posted as Eva felt like no 1 cares?

SayD: all de time

Groovechick2: u 2?

SayD: Mum says she cares but she don't listen – she jus hear

Groovechick2: u need 2 stop blaming her SayD

SayD: who?

Groovechick2: ur Ma

SayD: 4 wot?

Groovechick2: 4 no dad. 4 everything.

SayD: I blame her? How d u no I blame her?

Groovechick2: takes 1 2 no1. Take the power. Go out there and use ur power 4 good.

SayD: u sound like u play 2 much WoW

Groovechick2: that's why I'm on here

SayD: don't no how to use my power

Groovechick2: get the meangirlz. Find ur dad. Don't be scared

14

Standing up for Shonna

Thursday 27th September

Hairstyle: Updo

'Updo's are the classic solution to a bad hair day. Twist up
and secure with pins or a butterfly clip. Throw in a flower
accessory and just go wild!

When I woke up on Thursday morning, the first thing I
thought about was the Dads: 241, 254 and 278. Abraham
Smith, Charles Ward and Richard Swain-Coles. I felt as
if I had not stopped thinking about them for the last
fourteen hours. They were out there somewhere waking
up – just like me, but minus the Barbie wallpaper.

It was definitely a bad hair day so I tried out an updo,
replacing the flower with a feather accessory. It looked
OK, but disappointingly I didn't feel ready to 'go wild'.

'Maybe I *should* just email them,' I said to Billy on
our walk to school that morning. Since Shonna Matthews

stopped being my friend, Billy and I walk to school. It's kind of sad to walk to school with your geeky cousin, but not as sad as walking on your own.

But that morning Billy said nothing. He was rigidly silent.

'Well, what do you think?' I said.

'I'm too scared to say anything in case you yell at me again, Sadie,' said Billy. He had a point. I had bawled him out the night before with his 'helpful suggestion'.

'I'm sorry,' I said. 'I do value your opinion and I do need your help here.'

'Well, emailing them sounds like a start,' said Billy. 'There wasn't anything else on that PC that looked likely. I mean, we know that your ma definitely used fertility-in-touch.com and that she had a successful outcome – and you're it. It's got to be one of those three donors because we didn't find any others. By the way, your hair looks cool. I like the feather.'

He was right of course – about emailing the Dads, and about my hair looking cool come to that. But the idea of emailing three men who I didn't even know – didn't they warn you against that sort of stuff? I mean, I wouldn't go meet them on my own or in their houses obviously. I'm not an idiot – but still, the idea of emailing them was still as scary as hell. Not to mention that they might not know they were my dad.

'But what if they don't even know? What if Mum never told them?'

Billy was doing the humming thing again. 'Then I guess we'll meet them,' he said. 'If one of them is short with dark hair, blue streaks and a bad attitude then we'll know for sure.'

We were at the school gate now. Email later. Assembly first.

I stood three rows behind Tony Cruz, but with a perfect view of the back of his neck. There is an array of necks in Year Eleven, ranging from scrawny to spotty to bull neck. Tony's stands out by being muscular, but not too thick, and tanned. Billy was standing next to him and surprisingly he measured up well. He has his dad's dark skin and an elegant neck, but with broad shoulders too. I felt proud for him –his back view is really good. I must tell him.

So I guess my eyes were simply boring a hole in the back of Tony's skull which eventually he must have sensed because he turned round and looked directly at me. Like properly. I mean, Tony Cruz really looked at me. He raised his eyebrows in a kind of questioning way. After Wednesday night, I knew that he was really only a geek boy who carries memory sticks in his pocket. Nonetheless he was a geek boy with good muscle tone so I felt myself go very hot. I was sure my face was as red as a tomato.

He flashed a very tiny smile at me and turned back. I swear a row of Year Eight girls tittered. Then the dance team thundered on to the stage and did an unnecessary bump 'n' grind routine. I think Tony must like one of them – maybe Rada (she's the prettiest) – because his neck kept on going red, right up to his ears.

I found myself looking forward to lunch break already. I was going to tell him about emailing the dads, but he caught up with me before I'd even filed out of assembly and off to registration.

'Sadie!' he called, and a couple of girls from my class glanced round to see what was going on, wondering why Tony Cruz of all people was talking to that squirt Sadie Nathanson.

'How's it going?' He was doing the nodding thing as usual.

'Fine,' I said, 'and thanks for last night. It was pretty heavy finding that stuff.'

'No problem,' he said. 'I like the hair by the way. Feather looks cool.'

'Thanks.' I made a mental note to use this style again.

He beckoned me away from my class.

'Listen, I was talking to Billy,' he said quietly. 'He says Shonna Matthews has been really mean to you this term. I had you two pegged as best mates.'

I froze. Why was Tony so concerned about my friendship with Shonna all of a sudden?

'Yeah, well,' I said, trying to sound offhand, 'girls can be pretty mean.'

'I thought I might have a word with her,' said Tony. 'Tell her to lay off?'

It was like he was asking my permission. I was touched, but also surprised.

'Go right ahead,' I said. 'Talk to Shonna. Be my guest. Apparently she really likes you so if you have a word with her, she'll probably listen. But look out cos she does this thing where she talks really quiet . . . Then you have to lean in—'

'She does?' Tony interrupted me. 'She likes me? Shonna Matthews?'

'Yuh-huh! Duh?' I said, smacking my forehead with the heel of my hand.

Did he need constant reassurance that he was a magnet for just about all the girls in the school?

Then Tony did something really conceited. He giggled. He giggled and shook his head. Instead of the usual concerned nodding thing. It made me really angry that he could laugh at someone's feelings like that. Even if it was just Shonna's feelings – I mean, what if he laughed at me like that?

'Look,' I said, 'I hate Shonna Matthews, but she doesn't deserve to be laughed at.'

He kind of opened and shut his mouth, but there were no words so I carried on.

'Talk to her. Tell her to lay off giving me a hard time, but *don't laugh at her.*'

And I stalked off to registration, leaving him standing

there wordlessly staring, his mouth hanging ever so slightly open.

Dammit. I'd defended Shonna against Tony. What the hell was wrong with me? I couldn't quite let her go, could I? But why couldn't I stand up for myself in front of Shonna the way I'd just stood up for Shonna in front of Tony Cruz? Sometimes I scared myself. I was so weird.

15

How to Email Your Virtual Dad

The school library was generally not the most inspirational setting for even the dullest task – like writing a book report or revising for a biology exam. It was full of kids who didn't want to walk around a wet playground. They whispered and giggled to one another and passed notes. Then there were girlie swots trying to get some extra study in who would shush them every so often.

Luckily the sun was shining that day so most people had gone out of school to buy chips or to irritate the local shopkeepers.

So here I was in an empty library about to write an email to my dad who quite probably didn't even know I existed. My Virtual Dad.

Hello. I think I'm pretty sure you're my Dad. Do you remember 16 years ago Do you remember 16 years

ago when you registered with Fertility-in-touch.com?
Well, hello – I'm your daughter.

I looked up. Miss Frame, the librarian, was staring at me. It's a given, isn't it, that most teachers are social misfits from Planet Weird, but Miss Frame is probably the closest thing to a normal-person-who-happens-to-be-a-teacher that I've come across. She's sort of tidy-looking, with a neat figure and smart little clothes – like a china doll – and what she says is OK and surprising. Her hair is always changing too. She likes to try out a lot of different styles. That day she was sporting a Teddy girl style – very 1950s, pushed forward and secured with a clip. Totally retro. I think we must connect over our interest in hair because I can actually talk to Miss Frame in a funny sort of way.

'You look thoughtful, Sadie,' she said, and she smiled at me and went back to whatever it was that librarians do – stacking shelves, alphabetising, whatever.

'OK,' deep breath, 'I'm trying to write an email to my virtual dad,' I said. 'He doesn't know I exist.'

I don't know why I told her. But I guess it wasn't a secret. I didn't want it to be a secret. She probably knew anyway. Teachers gossip. She must have heard all about that human biology lesson in the staffroom.

Miss Frame didn't say anything for ages. Some teachers would have said, 'This is a study area, Ms Nathanson. This may be your lunch break, but the library is not an Internet café.' Or they might have drawn my attention to point C1(b) in the Student Internet Policy Handbook which was placed carefully next to every terminal:

You will not communicate with a stranger without your parent's approval.

Yeah, well, what if the 'stranger' you were communicating with WAS your parent? Guess they didn't have a clause that covered that.

Anyway, Miss Frame credited me with some level of intelligence because she didn't say any of these things. She was quiet for ages and then she said, 'I would imagine that's rather hard to do if you've never met him – if he doesn't know he has a daughter.'

'It *is* hard,' I said. 'I don't know how to start. I keep starting and it sounds ridiculous.'

So then Miss Frame put her books down and came over and sat on the edge of the desk, not so that she could see the screen, but so that she could see me. She has these real neat little hands and she sort of folded them so they were even neater. I could see her pearly pink nails and thin silver rings, and I looked down at my small inky, stubby, square fingers covered in hair dye. Who was I kidding? Tony Cruz couldn't like someone with these fingers.

Miss Frame smiled at me. 'Sadie, why don't you pretend you're talking to him? Why don't you write as if you're having a conversation?'

I couldn't do that. I just couldn't.

'Because I'm not having a conversation with him, am I?' I said. 'I'm sending him an email and I keep thinking about every single word I write and then I can't do it.'

I didn't tell her that I was also going to have to send it three times.

She stood up then and went back to her pile.

~~Dear Dad – this crazy librarian has advised me to write to you like we're having a conversation, which we're not.~~

I sat there for almost twenty minutes staring out of the window, until lunch break was practically over. Then Miss Frame put a book catalogue down and came over and perched on my desk again. She took a really deep breath in through her nose so that her neat little chest went up and down.

'OK,' she said, 'do you want to write this email to your dad?'

I stared at her. Maybe she was from Planet Weird after all. She was definitely on my case.

'Ye-es,' I said.

'Well, Sadie, then just write it. Write it. Just go blah blah blah on the computer and send it and then you've done it and you don't have to think about it any more!'

Then she unfolded her hands and smoothed her skirt down like she'd just given me her best apple pie recipe or taught me a new embroidery stitch.

'It's a courageous thing you've decided to do. It's bold. Be bold. After all, this isn't about the email you're sending – it's about the one you're going to get back, isn't it?'

'I guess.'

'If you don't send an email then you won't get a reply.'

'I guess.'

'So write it and send it.'

Then Miss Frame got up from the corner of the desk and went back to stacking and flicking through her catalogue.

Hi. I think you may be my Dad, according to this email I found that talks about this Disclosure Programme you registered for sixteen years ago, and this letter I have at home that you wrote to 'me' – or the virtual me. Anyway, I just want to say 'hi' and my name is Sadie and I just turned 15 and I'd like to

Then the end of lunch bell went. Dammit.

16

The Betrayal

It was difficult getting through the afternoon knowing that I still hadn't managed to send the emails. Now that I'd decided I was going to do it, I wanted it to be now. I wanted it to be yesterday.

As soon as the end-of-school bell went, I raced back to the library. I was hoping that nobody would be there so I could just concentrate on sending those emails – I was even hoping that Miss Frame wouldn't be there so she couldn't interrupt me.

The library appeared to be empty so I logged in and opened up my half-written email.

. . . get a reply from you really really soon - straight away in fact because it's quite nerve-wracking sending you this. Sadie Nathanson

I checked the addresses:

charles.ward2@hotmail.com

r.swaincoles@doctorsnet.org.uk

abe.smith@kent.gov.uk

And then I pressed *send* three times.

And then I watched it leave my outbox three times.

And then I checked Sent Items. And the emails were in there.

It made me feel really good to know I'd done it. That I'd started something.

And then I read what I'd written all over again and it sounded really lame – but you know what? Miss Frame was right – it wasn't about the message I'd sent, it was about the one I was going to get back.

My mum once told me she used to talk to herself whenever she was alone, and it was only after I was born that she realised she wasn't certifiable, but that she'd been talking to me all along. Well, I think that's what I realised after I sent that first message to my dad in Miss Frame's library that afternoon. All those imaginary conversations I'd had in my head – all that stuff about my dad looking over my shoulder – were real and there was nothing weird about any of it at all. All I needed now was for him to answer.

I logged out of my email and closed down the computer. Even the shut-down sound seemed to echo around the library. It felt as if everyone in the entire place had gone home. School can be a miserable place when it's full, but an empty school is like a collapsed lung. It was just me and some weird clanking pipe noises. It reminded me of Aunt Lilah's salon at night. All those dryers crying out for heads to put under them. All those magazines demanding to be read. I never stayed late at school if I could possibly help it – it creeped me out too much.

I went down the back stairs instead of out the front – I didn't want anyone to see me in case they asked me what I'd been doing or why I was still in school. I wanted to slip away home unnoticed, just to hold on to the feeling that I'd had when I sent those emails and not break its spell.

No such luck of course.

I was standing on the concrete steps outside the school building, the door handle in my hand, when I heard something from behind the enormous rubbish bins. Whispering. It was Shonna — she talks in this low whisper when she wants boys to lean towards her. *'It works every time, Sadie — you should try it. You talk quiet and they lean down towards you and they stare at your lips, and the next thing you know . . .'*

And I saw the back of the boy's neck, which I swear I could pick out now from any neck line-up. It was Tony's neck and he was straining forward towards her.

I had the door handle in my hand and I slammed the door as hard as I could. Then I ran. I ran past Tony and Shonna whispering and leaning behind those rubbish bins. His eyes on her lips *and the next thing you know . . . it works every time, Sadie — you should try it . . .* Tears blurred my eyes as I ran.

Lucky I know my way home blind.

Lilah's salon.

Mr Khan's.

The crossing.

The minimarket.

The 50p lady.

Home.

Mum's car was parked outside. She was in. There would be questions about why I was in tears so I had to

135

make a run for it. I flung open the door to the flat and charged through the lounge where Mum was sitting with her laptop, peering at a spreadsheet.

'Honey?'

'Homework,' I muttered before she could get up. I shut my bedroom door and flung myself under the duvet. Rabbi Rabbit muffled my sobs.

'Sadie, are you OK?' Mum was knocking on the door.

'HOMEWORK!!!!' I bellowed. Even in my distress I realised that I could take on Aunty Rita with that voice.

'OK OK.' I heard Mum go back into the lounge.

Tony Cruz. As if he'd been going to tell Shonna to 'lay off' me. Ha! How could I have fallen for that one? The way he'd giggled. The way he'd said, 'She likes me? Shonna Matthews?'

I should never have even . . .

Shonna Matthews. I hated her. I hated her even more if that was possible.

I stared down at my stubby, inky fingers and forced a laugh. I was laughing at myself. I mean, really – did I honestly think that Tony Cruz fancied me? Did I truly think for one moment that he felt anything other than pity for me? Pity because I was his best mate's cousin and I was small and quiet – like a little mouse on some quirky personal quest he'd been roped into.

I took a deep breath – like I'd seen Miss Frame do at lunchtime. Tony and Shonna were not going to ruin my day I decided. I would make myself not care. I would have poise. I would be self-contained. I would rely only on myself for everything. I stood up and looked in the mirror. The feather in my hair had bent over. I looked ridiculous.

I'd known all along that today was a bad hair day and I shouldn't have attempted a salvage operation. I went into the bathroom, switched on the shower and stepped under it.

'I am not going to ask,' said Mum when she saw me dripping on the mat in my school uniform. 'I am not going to yell because it might escalate and end in a double homicide.'

'Good,' I said, and then, 'I'll dry it all, OK.'

You know what, sometimes my Mum could be pretty cool about stuff that you wouldn't expect her to be cool about. Like getting my school uniform soaking wet.

'We won't say any more about it,' said Mum. 'We

won't even mention the fact that the blazer is *dry clean only*.'

And she didn't.

But now I just needed Mum to go to bed so I could check my emails on her laptop. Maybe Dad #241, #254 or #278 had emailed me. Unfortunately Mum was superglued to the laptop that night. I hung about, coming in and out of the lounge and staring at her, looking for an opportunity to nab the computer.

'Are you all right, love?' she asked finally. 'You seem restless.' She was flicking through her Rolodex now, her elbow resting on the laptop. 'You look pale too.'

It was tempting to say I was ill – just to make Mum feel better. She's always convinced I'm ill or about to be ill. She's never happier it seems than when she's taking my temperature or warming up hot lemon and honey. But I decided not to humour her.

'I'm fine,' I said. 'Just loads of study I'm avoiding, that's all. It's all fine. All under control.'

She put her arm round me and gave me a hug. I do love my mum and it was so tempting, when there was just the two of us, to tell her everything: about Tony and Shonna, about the Dads. But she wouldn't have solved

138

any of it quietly. It's not like it would stay just between the two of us, like a normal Mother/Daughter thing. She would immediately overreact and involve everyone. She'd get Uncle Zé over to cook and Aunt Lilah to have hysterics and Great Aunty Rita to shout at everyone. I needed to deal with everything on my own so I resisted the urge to blab.

Instead of a heart-to-heart I reached for the remote and put on the telly. I could feel the hot tears starting to prick my eyes again whenever I thought about school and Tony and Shonna. Then *Good as it Gets: Behind the Scenes* — a spin-off from the Tuesday night programme — was about to kick off and Aunt Lilah was ringing the buzzer.

'It's Thursday!' said Mum. 'It must be Thursday!'

When I'm a grown-up, if you can pin my life and my whereabouts down to what's on the telly, then somebody shoot me and put me out of my misery. Aunt Lilah was 'yoo-hooing' up the stairs because it was Thursday and time for the spin-off of her favourite programme and she had no one to appreciate it with round at hers. It was tragic really, but it was also diverting and so this time I didn't storm off to my room. I sat next to Mum instead and we made faces at each other behind Aunt

Lilah's back, and actually laughed at people who thought they could sing, but were tone-deaf, and people who thought they could dance, but had two left feet.

'That was extraordinary!' said Harry 'The Hurricane' Hodder, the awful judge, after someone in beige had wailed her way through 'My Heart will Go On'.

'Thanks,' said the Beige One.

'No — I don't mean it as a compliment. It was seriously weird. You sounded as if you were yelling at your neighbour.'

Aunt Lilah practically pulled a muscle laughing at that one.

Later, when Aunt Lilah had gone — giggling all the way home at The Hurricane's put-downs — and Mum was in bed, ear plugs in, dead to the world, I nipped out of bed and logged onto the laptop. There were two emails waiting for me.

This message was created automatically by mail delivery software. A message that you sent could not be delivered to one or more of its recipients. This is a permanent error. The following address(es) failed:
charles.ward2@hotmail.com

Catastrophe.

And worse.

This message was created automatically by mail delivery software. A message that you sent could not be delivered to one or more of its recipients. This is a permanent error. The following address(es) failed:

r.swaincoles@doctorsnet.org.uk

There are some days when you shouldn't even bother to get out of bed. My hair had been trying to tell me that all day and I'd ignored it. I'd even tried to wash that man right out of it, like that stupid old song says. Never ignore your hair. It's like a gauge for what kind of day you're about to have.

Current Mood: Took the power; crashed&burned

Groovechick2: huh?

SayD: 2 x dads down in flames & it turns out nodding guy likes meangirlz & I hv ugly hands

Groovechick2: OMG ur life sux 2day girl

SayD: & the news? Feel like duvet diving 4ever

Groovechick2: dn't do it. keep going. dn't let thm win

SayD: wanna cry. I dn't no y they hate me so much & how he cd be so mean 2 me 2. I trusted him wiv the dad stuff and he betrayed me

Groovechick2: u don't need them – any of them. Ur betta than them

SayD: Feel like they're winning. sniff

Groovechick2: don't let em win. Believe in urself. Stand up to em. Find ur dad

SayD: how's u?

Groovechick2: same old. I = homework boyf = WoW

SayD: wish I still liked BarB. wish I was 6 y.o. and still liked my ma

Groovechick2: funny; 1 day you wake up & everything they say = annoying

SayD: & everything they don't say 2

17

Googling the Dads

Friday 28th September
Hairstyle: Basket-weave Braid
This is a tricky one to pull off on your own so you'll need a friend to assist in the creation of this stand-out fabulous braid. You'll also need twenty minutes, shoulder-length to long straight hair or clip-in extensions, a styling comb and a scrunchie. You'll be sleek and stylish without a hair out of place!

'I thought this might happen,' said Billy after Friday night tea.

I had spent the day with a face like an emo, avoiding everyone. Now I was lying on his bunk bemoaning the undeliverable emails at the same time as feeling down the sides of the bed for any stray pictures of Shonna that I might have missed.

'So who's left?' said Billy.

'Abraham Smith – municipal gardener from Kent,' I said. 'Come in number 241 – your kid is desperate.'

'Well, it's not all bad news then,' said Billy.

'How d'you mean?' I was instantly irritated.

I couldn't quite see how this failed to qualify as bad news. I mean, our line of enquiry was two-thirds dead in the water as of yesterday evening.

'Well,' said Billy, 'like I say – I thought this might happen and so I've been doing some research.'

I sat up in the bunk and peered over at him.

'What kind of research?'

'Just Internet – just Googling.'

'And?'

'And and and . . .' said Billy, 'Dad number 278 – Richard Swain-Coles – *is* a doctor. It was really easy to find him. All doctors are on a register somewhere and his name's pretty unusual. There can't be two doctors with that name in this country.'

'Wooooo! This is big,' I said. 'You mean, you've found him?'

'Yuh-huh. Like I said, it was easy. I'll show you.'

He turned round to face his computer while I hopped down from the bunk. *Click click* and we were in a website entitled *Swain-Coles Cosmetic Surgery* with some shopping mall music playing in the background, presumably to calm you down while you considered having: *The breasts you've always wanted from £77 a month*. Another click revealed a photograph of a tall dark man sitting behind a mahogany desk, smiling into the camera. The elaborate signature of Richard Swain-Coles cut across the image.

Winston Churchill Baby? Could be.

Worry crinkle? It was impossible to tell.

But there was an email address and a form to fill out to register for a consultation. *Click click* and Billy was in the form.

'I've done a full spread,' he said. 'I put you down for cheek implants, Botox, ear correction and liposuction from the buttock area. I just want to make sure you only see Dr Swain-Coles and no one junior or a specialist plastic surgeon or something.'

I thought about the red book from Mum's Special Box.

'I had unequal buttock size when I was a baby,' I said. I mentioned this simply because I was too freaked to think of anything else to say and it seemed oddly relevant.

'Excellent,' said Billy. 'Shall we send?'

'Hold on,' I said.

'What?' said Billy. 'What's the problem?'

'It's just . . . it's just all moving so fast. I mean, I want it to, but . . . y'know?'

Billy raised his eyebrows. 'Send? Shall I? Send? Shall I?' On and on like a stuck record, his mouse poised above the button.

'I guess,' I said eventually.

'I'll request a consultation then?'

'I guess,' I said.

'Oh good,' said Billy. 'Because I did it last night and they've already confirmed your appointment.'

'You did what? They did what?'

'Didn't want to hang about – I mean, we could have cancelled it if you decided not to, but I just thought . . .'

'It's fine,' I said. 'You've requested the appointment. They've confirmed. I've a full consultation on having my entire body fat taken from one side and squeezed into somewhere else – and all in the name of "trying to find my dad".'

'Is it OK? Would you like me to cancel?' said Billy. He looked concerned. 'I mean, I'll be with you obviously. You won't have to go alone.'

'No, it's fine,' I said. 'Of course, the whole thing is insane, but on some level of insanity it's fine as well. Dr Swain-Coles might be my dad and maybe he can line up my buns as a father-daughter bonding exercise.'

'It's four-thirty on Tuesday,' continued Billy, ignoring my rant. 'Gives us an hour to get to West London from school. Oh, and you're eighteen not fifteen as well.'

Everything was indeed moving very fast and something was bothering me.

'Billy, is there any reason why we couldn't just have found a current email address for Dr Swain-Coles and told him the real reason we wanted to see him, instead of pretending I need cosmetic surgery?'

Billy was quiet for a moment.

'Y'know what?' he said. 'In a way it was a good thing that we didn't hear back from these two guys on their original emails, because if we go undercover, we get to check them out first. I mean, you may take one look and run in the opposite direction – you may not want to share your genetic heritage with any of them.'

He was right, I suppose. I'd never really thought about the possibility of not actually liking my dad – I'd fantasised about meeting him for so long. But I might take one look at Richard Swain-Coles's worry crinkle and not want to match it with my own at all. I might just want to walk out of there and never say another word to him.

'Did you do anything else last night, Billy?' I asked. 'For instance, have you got Charles Ward hidden under your mattress next to your dodgy guitar mags?'

Nothing would surprise me now.

"Dad number 254, Charles Ward, is proving to be more difficult,' said Billy.

I wasn't sure whether to be relieved or disappointed. I wasn't sure I could take any more surprises.

'Charles Ward stated his occupation as actor,' Billy went on, 'but he's clearly not famous because I can't trace him under that name.'

'Oh, so that's that then,' I said. We had lost #254. Yet #278 had been so easy! 'But we can't give up,' I said. 'What if Charles Ward is the one?'

'We do have one more line of enquiry,' said Billy.

'Oh?'

'Equity,' said Billy. 'It's the union that all actors are members of.'

'Oh,' I said. 'I can't see how that's going to . . .'

'And they can forward mail to their members' addresses for you.'

'OK, now I see.'

'So we just have to write a letter – something formal and businesslike, printed out on nice paper, but something that'll definitely get his attention. Like mentioning the feritility-in-touch.com site.'

'I'm guessing that'll get his attention,' I said. 'Might also induce a heart attack. What's the excuse for meeting him though?'

Billy sat with his head in his hands for some time. He was doing the humming thing. 'I know,' he said eventually. 'You're a journalist doing an article on sperm donors.'

'And ask him to meet us?'

'Ask him to meet you, but I'll be there as well, obviously.'

'Really? I'd kind of like to do this on my own, but–'

'Don't be an idiot,' said Billy. 'I'm coming with you whether you like it or not.'

There really was a part of me that wanted to do this alone, but I was secretly relieved at Billy's insistence on being there.

Dear Mr Ward

I would like to meet with you to discuss a website called Fertility-In-Touch.com. I'm writing a newspaper article on sperm donation and I believe you had a connection to this site some years ago.

I suggest meeting at

'Where shall we meet him? We can't very well get him to come here, can we?'

'Somewhere public,' said Billy. 'Safer, and it'll seem more like a proper business meeting.'

'But where?' I couldn't imagine where people had proper business meetings.

Billy rifled through the pile of papers he'd printed out from his investigations. While he did that, I checked his hair. He'd dried it too flat. It needed something – lift? Gel?

'Here we are,' he said, 'Equity's offices. It says here "we have a waiting room which can serve as an informal meeting place for our members." Let's say we'll meet him there. Nice and central. Very businesslike.'

I suggest meeting at Equity's head office in St Martin's Lane for a discussion at 4.30 p.m. on Thursday 4th October.

Yours

S. Nathanson

I put down the number from my old mobile at the bottom of the letter, because that seemed more businesslike too. I still had the phone and the number, and I figured it would be better than giving him my current number. But something was bothering me.

'Billy, he'll never think we're journalists. You're nearly sixteen years old, and have you looked at me? I can barely pass for twelve. He's never going to believe us.'

'It doesn't matter how we look,' said Billy. 'By the time Charles Ward spots us, we'll have spotted him first, and you'll have decided whether you want to meet him or not. If you do, then you can just tell him the real reason we're there.'

That made sense.

It was weird sending off an actual printed letter. I don't think I've ever done that before. I tucked it into

151

the envelope, stuck on one of Aunt Lilah's stamps, then Billy walked me to the postbox. We watched the small white letter disappear into the black hole and to who knows where. It felt like a historic moment – quite unlike emailing.

'That's it then,' said Billy. 'It's gone.'

'I'll pop round tomorrow afternoon and sort your hair,' I said.

'What's up with it?'

'It's not quite right,' I said. 'You've dried it too flat.'

18

When Do Boys Start to Get Nice?

Saturday afternoon I washed Billy's hair, towelled it, then realised that it needed a bit of a tidy too. So I was on my way down to the salon for some scissors when I almost collided with Tony Cruz, who was on his way up to Billy's room. The image of him and Shonna behind the bins zoomed back into my head with a crash.

'*They lean down towards you and the next thing you know . . .*'

Tracking down my dads with Billy had almost made me forget the whole sickening episode, but I hadn't really. I'd just put the memory on pause. I *had* seen Tony and Shonna on Thursday night and they'd made me feel like I was nothing. And here he was, bold as you like, on his way up to Billy's room – with his bobbing *malaki ulo* (Uncle-speak for 'big head'). Really, he had swagger.

That was until he clocked me and then he kind of straightened up and took his hands out of his pockets. I looked right down as if he wasn't there – which of course was ridiculous because he was like one millimetre from my face.

'Sadie?' he said. 'Are you–?'

He was all concern. Like nothing had ever happened. I stormed past him before he even had time to finish his sentence, slamming the door at the bottom of the stairs as I went. I couldn't help checking my Basket-weave Braid in one of the salon mirrors as I went by though. I'd managed to create it all by myself, thank you very much, and it had lasted two whole days. I needed to know that it was holding up to the trauma of my recent life. It was. Unfortunately my worry crinkle had appeared.

Now I could hear footsteps behind me. Tony? Perhaps he was coming after me. Perhaps he was going to apologise, explain . . .

I turned and saw Uncle Zé coming through to the shop.

He peered at me. 'Everything OK there, my *anak*?'

'No,' I scowled.

'Thought the door was about to leave its hinges then.'

'Sorry, *tito*.'

My lip started to quiver because I was thinking of Shonna and Tony again. On Monday Shonna and Imelda would be laughing at me. Shonna would say, 'Did you actually think Tony Cruz was even slightly interested in you? Ha! Don't make me laugh. He was just winding you up. He doesn't date dwarves. He thinks you're an idiot.'

Oh yeah, I could see exactly how this was going to go.

'Come here, *anak*,' said Uncle Zé, and he held out his arms to me. Of course when people are kind, it always makes you feel so much worse. The next thing I was blubbing and sniffing into his chef's apron, which always smelled deliciously of roasted pork crackling.

'Don't get wound up over boys,' said Uncle Zé. 'They're *chooches*, *bobos* — *idyotas*. Believe me, they're not even worth bothering with.'

'I'm not getting w-w-wound up over boys,' I half-lied.

'Well, whatever it is, it's not worth it. He, she or it. Try forget about it. Here — five bucks for you, *anak*.' He thrust a five-pound note at me. 'Put it towards

155

something. There are sales on — put it with your birthday money and treat yourself.'

'You don't have to, *tito*,' I said.

'I know,' he said, 'but I want to.'

When do boys start to get nice like Uncle? Are they really all *idyotas* and *bobos* like he said? Mum says Aunt Lilah got the only good man. I think she may be right. It made me wonder what if Mum had married Uncle Zé and he was my dad. Would my life be any better? It would be less complicated. But then there'd be no Billy too.

I headed for the park. I needed space to get my thoughts in order. I had a momentary pang as I remembered Billy was still waiting for me up in the flat, his hair dripping down into his eyes. He would sit there for ages before he realised I'd legged it. My last words to him were, 'Don't move — under pain of death.'

By the time I got to the park I had two missed calls on my phone and a text message. The calls were Billy's — probably wondering where the hell I was. The text was from a number I didn't recognise. It said: **r u ok? Wossup? Tony**

Tony Cruz had my number. He was texting me.

I ignored him and I ignored Billy too.

It was drizzling now. The sky was a nasty grey and the streets looked dirty and ruined. I had no umbrella so I was glad I'd opted for the braid. It wouldn't spoil in the wet.

The 50p lady walked by with a grin on her face. She was carrying two ice creams and the rain was making dents in their perfectly whipped tops. I made my way into the deserted little playground at the corner of the park and sat on the roundabout. I used to come to this playground every single day after school. At one point I think I imagined it was *my* playground. It was a shabby little spot really, uncared for and graffitied. There were piles of fag butts at the foot of the slide from where older kids sat at night and smoked.

Somewhere in my life this playground had been the focus of all my greatest adventures and games. Shonna and I would lie on this roundabout – our heads on the footplates and our feet draped over the seats – and we would talk for hours, while other children jumped on and off and spun us faster and faster. We would talk about how we wanted to be pop stars or hairdressers or vets, and who we would marry and how many children we would have and what their names would be, and how many bridesmaids and what our husbands would look like. And when we'd finished talking about our husbands, we'd talk about our dads and how they were firemen or maybe soldiers – because we were quite sure that whatever they were, they were terribly brave.

You see the funny thing is that Shonna doesn't have a dad either. Well, of course she has a dad in the way that everyone on this earth has a dad. But Shonna never knew her dad, had never really seen him. Shonna's mum and dad had been in high school together. They got married when Jeanette was sixteen and then, when Shonna was just a baby, her dad disappeared. He went down the betting shop on the corner of Park Road one winter afternoon and he never came back. So from day one Shonna and I were united in our Dadlessness.

I always found it odd when Shonna told that story that no one in her family had ever thought to go out looking for him. And if Shonna mentioned her dad within earshot of home, her nan would always take a sharp drag on her cigarette and mutter, 'Did us all a favour by disappearing if you ask me.' Really, nobody seemed to care that he'd vanished except Shonna, who wondered and wondered about him.

And then one day, when we'd just started in Year Nine, he came back again. Well, he didn't come back to Jeanette, but someone said they'd seen him down on Bethnal Green Road and someone else said he drank in The Blind Beggar at Whitechapel. Before we knew it, Shonna and I were on the 388 bus down to Bethnal Green, walking up and down with a blurry photo taken fifteen years previously, trying to match it up with the faces of the middle-aged men on the streets. We even popped our heads into one of the dodgy old-man pubs down where Shonna's uncles drank. They made the same faces as her nan. They said they hadn't seen him, but they looked shifty about it.

And then last March, just after Shonna turned fourteen and she had birthday money to burn, we went round Whitechapel Market looking for cheap glittery shoes. We went in McDonald's for a shake and that's when we saw the old trampy guy. He was sitting by the window and he kept looking over at us. He was wearing this dirty coat and his skin had like a film of brown over it – it reminded me of the inside of a teapot. He was rolling a ciggie and you could see that his nails were filthy.

Well, I was all for ignoring him, which is what you do with the crazies – you pretend they aren't there, you don't make eye contact and then they don't bother you. But Shonna kept looking over at this old guy the whole time, like she knew him. And then something horrible happened. The old filthy tramp smiled at her so that we could see all his brown crumbly teeth and then he called her name.

Without any warning at all, Shonna jumped up so fast that she knocked over her chair and ran out of McDonald's leaving her shake sitting on the table. I had to run to catch her up. She was frantically flagging down a bus. While I was running, I was thinking, *What the hell's she doing? Why are we running? Who was that guy? How did he know her name?*

And then I realised like this great light bulb going on over my head – *that* was her dad. That old dirty man with the filthy fingernails was Shonna's dad. He wasn't in the army or the fire brigade. He was down and out. Sleeping rough.

When the bus opened its doors, Shonna ran straight up to the top deck without even looking to see if I was behind her. Then she sat in the outside seat and turned her head towards the window and put her earbuds in for her MP3. I got the message that she didn't want me around, so I went downstairs with the two milkshakes and we never said anything to each other about it when we got off the bus at the same stop. In fact, we never said anything to each other about anything because Shonna kept her earbuds in right until we got to Aunt Lilah's salon.

That was when I said something I shouldn't have. What I really wanted to do was to hug Shonna and tell her how awful I felt about that old trampy guy being her dad, but in that moment outside the salon she made me feel as if I didn't have any right. And the way she'd just run away from me at McDonald's, and made me sit on the bus all on my own. And the way she just wouldn't talk to me and had always been better at stuff like making a joke of everything and getting people to like her. And suddenly, just this once, I was the one with the advantage. I still hadn't found *my* dad. *My* dad still had infinite possibilities of greatness.

So I said it. We were outside Aunt Lilah's shop and I just said it. I said, 'I'm thinking about trying to trace my dad.'

I don't know why I did it. For all the above reasons I guess. I could kick myself for it now. It was so wrong. She must have felt as if I was rubbing salt in the wound because all those fantasies we'd had in the playground lying on the roundabout – none of them applied to Shonna's dad any more.

Shonna never said anything. She just kicked the brickwork under the shop window. Then she turned to go and her face looked kind of set. Her mouth was a perfectly straight line.

'Laters,' I called after her. But she never even looked back.

The next day she outed me in Mr Graves's human biology lesson and on my fifteenth birthday she sent me a fake birthday card from my dad. I guess in some ways I deserved it.

19

Standing up to Shonna

Monday 1st October

Hairstyle: Feisty Facelift Pony

This ponytail is worn as tight as you dare at the top of the head, giving the effect of a facelift. It's sporty, it's cheeky, it's really feisty and it's guaranteed to iron out all your wrinkles! Use anti-frizz serum to 'glue' the hair flat and give it a sleek, shiny finish. You can make this more feminine by bringing stray tendrils down around the ears for a softening effect.

OK, I admit it; I always start off the week hoping somewhere deep down that Shonna Matthews will turn round and smile at me like she used to when she was my best friend. But of course that'll never happen. In fact, first period Monday morning, outside the maths room, they were waiting for me: Shonna and Imelda. Mr Stone was late for class as usual so, while I queued with the other dopey kids, all shouting and giggling and talking about who was going to win *Good as it Gets* this series, Shonna and Imelda took it in turns to kick the back of my school skirt.

'Oops, sorry,' said Imelda, 'I thought you was the doormat.'

Kick.

'Bit stinky for a doormat. I don't think I'd want to wipe my shoes on that,' said Shonna.

Kick.

Anger rose in my throat. I hated Shonna Matthews. She'd gone in for the kill with Tony just to spite me.

'You know she thinks she's cool because she hangs out with a band. Bunch of lamers.'

Kick.

I hated Shonna Matthews. She was mean about my cousin Billy.

He's creeping me out, Sadie. I don't mean to be rude, but it's a bit freaky.

Kick.

I hated Shonna Matthews. She'd sent me that fake birthday card.

Kick. Kick. Kick.

Someone opened the classroom door and there was a rush behind me. A hand grabbed my ponytail and yanked it hard. My back stiffened and some other force seemed to seize control of me. At that moment I loathed Shonna Matthews completely and utterly. I didn't want her to smile at me like she used to when she was my best friend. I just wanted to pulverise her. I was going to forget my zero combat rating and I WASN'T GOING TO BE BULLIED BY HER ANY MORE.

Groovechick2's words of wisdom rang in my ears: don't let em win. Believe in urself. Stand up to em. Find ur dad.

I turned round and faced my enemy. Full on. So that she couldn't ignore me and she couldn't get by me either. I was blocking her between two of the desks. She was trapped.

'You think I hang out with a bunch of lamers?' I asked.

'Wha'ever, Sadie,' said Shonna, like she wasn't even bothered at all.

'Have you *seen* your mate over there?' And I gestured at Imelda, who started to protest.

'What the—?'

'Yeah, you with the squashed face,' I said to Imelda. 'What happened to your head – did your mum drop you? Do you sleep in a vice?'

Someone else in the classroom gasped.

'Are you having a laugh?' said Imelda. She was struggling to get to me, but Shonna was in the way, wedged between me and the desks.

'Oh my God, Sadie, you've done it now!' said Dena Barbulis behind me.

'You poison dwarf!' said Shonna, and she leaned towards me and poked me in the chest with her bony finger. 'How dare you say that to her?' Her chin jutted into my face and bits of saliva sprayed me, she was leaning in so close. She reminded me of a hissing cat.

I drew back. 'Keep away from me,' I said. 'There's something crawling in your hair.'

'You what?!'

'Shonna, you do have to wash it sometimes, y'know.'

'What is your problem?' said Shonna, and she shoved me hard. 'You are getting right on my wick.'

'Yeah,' said Imelda. She leaned over Shonna and yanked my pony tail, wrenching the hair from its roots again.

I didn't even cry out – in fact, I was enjoying it. All of it.

'Oh my God!' said Dena again. 'You're gonna get it, Sadie!'

But now that I'd started I couldn't stop. I was on some kind of retaliation rollercoaster and it felt totally liberating. I sank my fingernails into Imelda's arm – the arm that was pulling my hair.

'Ow, you skank!' she shrieked.

'The only reason Shonna hangs out with you,' I said as she tried to wrench free, 'is because you're so thick you just do as you're told.'

Then several things seemed to happen at once.

Shonna screamed at me, 'Shut it, just shut it!'

Imelda took a flying leap over the desk and grabbed for my arm trying to yank it up my back.

People in the classroom chanted, 'Cat fight! Cat fight!'

The blood rushed to my head and I yelled, fast and loud:

'Palabok langhap sarap! Macapuno!

Longganisa Longganisa!

Love ko 'to! Love ko 'to! Love ko 'to!'

167

Shonna backed away from me, but I kept going at her. She was caught between me and the rest of the class who were still chanting. Imelda was behind, grabbing at my arm.

I was so close to Shonna that I could see the pores on her cheeks and the little cluster of blackheads around her nose. *Your skin is bad, man*, is what I thought as I yelled.

'*Macapuno! Longganisa!*'

She must have thought I was really cursing at her, when actually I was reciting a menu from this fast-food place in the Philippines called Jollibee that Billy and I learned off by heart one year. When you shouted the words over and over – and I really did bawl them into Shonna's face – it sounded fierce.

'Let's calm it down,' said Kip, who was pushing his way into the room, clambering over the desks to reach us.

Mr Stone followed close behind. I could see that he was not impressed by any of it as he came level with us.

'What in God's name do you think you're doing, girls?'

I stared at him. I stared at Shonna. She was purple in

the face with rage. I guess I probably looked the same, but I was damned if I was going to wait around to be sent to the headmaster, to be told I should be ashamed of myself, that I'd let the school and myself down and every other stupid cliché under the sun.

So I did the other thing I'd wanted to do for a long time. I just walked out of class.

20

U OK?

I guess it was a kind of juvenile, girlie thing to do, but it felt right on a very wrong sort of day, so I kept on walking, out of the class and right out of school.

I could hear Mr Stone calling after me: 'Sadie Nathanson! Come here, we need to sort this out!' But he couldn't stop me. He was not going to stop me. I kept right on walking until I could no longer see the school and I could breathe again. The park came into view, the Beigal shop, the Fish House, the minimart and then the bottom of my road.

I checked my watch – 10 a.m. It felt as if a great deal had happened, but it turned out that only one hour of school had actually passed. So much drama. So little time.

Mum wasn't home when I stomped into the flat. I was still on a bit of a high from the fight with Shonna and marching out of school. Without a pass. Without permission. And during a lesson. I couldn't help smiling even though the chances were I'd be totally punished by the school and by Mum. But hadn't I just stood up to Shonna Matthews finally after months of her bitching at me? Any amount of detention, grounding or earbashing would be completely worth it.

All that 'cursing' the Jollibee menu had made me hungry. I poured myself a bowl of Cheerios and then another and then another. I was starving.

From inside my bag I heard my phone buzz. Two texts.

Billy: U OK?

U OK? Tony

Clearly news travels fast.

I had to laugh out loud at the second one. A high pitched 'Ha!' and then, as it was a day for standing up for myself, I texted Tony right back.

SD: Yes I loved c·ing u x my nme. SADIE

I didn't know why Tony Cruz was texting me, but I was pretty sure it wasn't to check on my welfare. Maybe Shonna had put him up to it – another way of tormenting me. I needed to zone out, so I sat down on the sofa with another bowl of Cheerios and switched on daytime television. A woman with very big hair was interviewing Harry 'The Hurricane' Hodder. The man was everywhere! I wasn't interested in Harry Hodder, but I was quite fascinated by the woman's hair. How did she get it that tall? Did she have a Bumpit under there or was it all backcombing and hairspray?

The doorbell went. I had half a mind not to answer it. It was probably the postman delivering a package for one of the neighbours and just trying all the buttons. Then again, there was always a chance it was something for me. I pressed the 'greet' button.

'Who is it?'

'Hi,' said Tony Cruz.

There's a camera on our entry phone and now I peered at the monitor. Sure enough I could see Tony standing outside the metal doors. He looked kind of forlorn. I couldn't see the blue of his eyes on that image, and I couldn't sense his amazing positivity from all that nodding. In fact, his head looked still.

'What d'you want?' I said. I felt buzzed from the fight again and I was suddenly outraged that Tony Cruz was round here ringing *my* doorbell.

'I need to talk to you . . .'

The temptation to just leave him standing outside was very great. The temptation to open the window above the front porch and throw a bucket of slime over him was even greater. But there was this other part of me that was curious to know what had brought him round here. What could he possibly have to say to me after the other night behind the bins?

'I'll come down,' I said.

On the way out I checked my hair in the hall mirror. My Facelift Pony was looking a bit dishevelled from where Imelda had been yanking it earlier. I took the elastic out. If you want the truth, that hairstyle was giving me a headache and I didn't know how people could put up with it all day. My eyebrows couldn't take that kind of pressure. I picked up my hairbrush and smoothed the hair back down.

Instead of using the lift, I went by the stairs, deliberately taking my time. *Slowly, slowly now. Not too fast. You don't know what he wants. Probably just wants to vex you again.*

He was standing there, his hands in the back pockets of his jeans. He had on a thin T-shirt and I could see goosebumps on his tanned arms. He took his hands out of his pockets when he saw me and made a sort of shrugging gesture.

'It's just me,' he said, like he was apologising.

'Hello, *just me*,' I said as flatly as I could. 'What's going on?'

'Can we talk somewhere? It feels kind of public out here. Your neighbours might be listening.'

Unlikely.

'My neighbours are all at work, Tony.' It was weird how I wasn't gabbling at him. I spoke slowly and deliberately like I didn't care, like I was bored actually. No Total Boy Paralysis today.

'I've got a home-study period and I can't concentrate,' said Tony. 'I just wanted to clear up all this mess between us.'

'What mess? You and Shonna behind the bins didn't look like a mess to me. You looked like you were having a fine old time.'

'Huh?' He shook his head like he didn't know what I was talking about. 'You cut me dead the other day over at Billy's and you slammed the door when you saw me talking to Shonna by the bins. And why did you send me that text just now? I don't understand it.'

174

Who was he kidding?

'Tony, I'm not an idiot. I know what I saw.'

'Sadie, I told you I was going to talk to Shonna and that's exactly what I was doing. Talking to her. I don't see what the deal is here. I was defending you. I was trying to be nice.'

'Well, that wasn't what it looked like.'

'Well, that's what it was.'

Tony shook his head. Then he said, 'Come on, Sadie. Just let me explain.' And he held out his hand to me.

It felt quite natural to take his hand. If something can feel thrilling and natural at the same time. He sort of tugged me out of the car park and then we ran so fast that I was giggling as we seemed to be flying by the Fish House and the Beigal shop. And then Tony did one of those boy things – he vaulted the park railings in two moves and waited for me to do the same.

Of course I couldn't. I clambered about lamely on one side, so he came back over and gave me a leg-up halfway and then leaped over to the other side to lift me down. It seemed to take forever, the lifting down. It was like we were moving in slow motion. Tony stood in front of me and put his arms out, and first I leaned the

175

wrong way and we bumped heads and laughed, and then we got it right and he lifted me down gracefully. Really, it was elegant. I was conscious of everything: my weight, his arms, the cold air. And then once we were on the other side of the railings, we stood awkwardly looking at one another. The high of the last few minutes died down and I remembered how angry I was with him.

'Tony, what're we doing here?' I asked very quietly. I mean, I needed to be clear when I was around him. He blurred everything, plus he was doing his leaning thing – this time against the railings, and closing his eyes. I tried not to let it bother me. I liked the leaning thing a lot. Too much. I needed to retain my anger.

'We're talking,' said Tony. He took my hand again and led me into the kids' playground.

I hadn't been in this playground for five years or more, and now weirdly this was the second time in a week. I sat gently on the seat of the seesaw. A little girl dressed in orange was on the other end and, as I sat down, she rose slowly into the air. She pointed at me.

'You're too big for the thee-thaw,' she said.

I smiled at her and then Tony sat in the middle of the

see-saw facing me, with his legs dangling either side of the pivot. My pulse raced. I could feel my hand tingling where he'd been holding it.

'You obviously think I've done something really, really heinous and I haven't, Sadie, and I want to sort this before you think I'm . . . a jerk or what your Uncle Zé would call a *chooch* or something.'

He was right. When I thought about Thursday night behind the bins, I did think Tony was a *chooch* and a *bobo* and an *idyota*.

'I don't know what you think was going on with me and Shonna, but it was NOTHING. You have to believe me,' said Tony gravely. He looked me straight in the eye.

'Oi,' said the Orange Girl from behind Tony, 'are you teenagerth?'

I smiled at her and nodded. Tony turned round.

'Yes,' he said to the girl. 'Are you a teenager?'

She howled with laughter. 'Don't be thilly, I'm four,' she said.

He turned back to me and looked serious. 'Do you believe me?'

'You are too big for the thee-thaw,' insisted the Orange Girl. 'You're teenagerth.'

177

So we bounced the see-saw up and down a bit to give her a ride.

'I need a wee now,' she said after a while. I let her down, then got off and pointed her in the direction of her minder. When I turned back, Tony was standing up in the middle of the see-saw and was walking along it from one end to the other.

'You have to believe me,' he said. 'I was only doing what I said I'd do. I was telling Shonna to leave you alone.'

He *had* said he'd talk to Shonna. That bit was true.

'That might have been your intention,' I said, 'but that wasn't what it *looked* like!' No. When it came down to it, I just didn't believe him. 'It looked really . . . intimate.'

He jumped down, picked up one end of the see-saw and straddled the seat, holding it up between his thighs. Because I'm such a shrimp I had to force the other end down to climb into position. I pushed it down too hard and Tony's end bounced up and caught him in the nuts. The colour drained from his face and he gripped the handles of the see-saw as if he was on a white-knuckle ride and not just in a kids' playground.

'Wow, that hurt!' he said. 'Takes your breath away.'

'Sorry,' I said, wishing I was dead.

'Whooooooo!' said Tony. He was shaking his head now.

He did some breathing. Short breaths out. One long breath in.

I was still mad at him and I still had to make my point even if I had just gravely injured him.

'I'm sorry, Tony, but you didn't look like you were "just talking" to Shonna – not from where I was standing!'

What kind of a dummy did he think I was? I jumped off the see-saw and the suddenness of the movement surprised him. The other end dropped to the ground, hitting Tony on the ankle as it fell. He gasped and clutched his foot.

Someone just kill me now, please.

I couldn't think of anything to say apart from, 'Would you like me to phone for an ambulance?' so I started walking back to the playground entrance. I could hear Tony running behind me, limping slightly and wheezing.

'Sadie! Wait!'

I turned to face him.

'Your friend – your ex-friend – is . . . very . . .'

My blood froze.

'What? She's very what?'

What was he trying to say? That Shonna was pretty, exciting, alluring?

'Scary,' he said finally.

'Scary?' He was scared of Shonna Matthews?

'Yuh.' He was doing the nodding thing now. 'She's intimidating. You were right and I wish I'd listened to you – that thing she does that you told me about? I kept saying "pardon" and "what", and I had to lean towards her. I thought she was going to jump me or something.'

'I warned you – she totally does it on purpose,' I said. 'Then she lunges. She says it never fails.'

'Well, it did fail. It failed with me and I told her to lay off you too.'

He sat down at my feet and peeled back his sock. The see-saw had broken the skin on his ankle. I knelt down next to him. Maybe, just maybe, he *was* telling me the truth. I'd tried to defend myself against his lies, but maybe they weren't lies. Tony Cruz found Shonna 'intimidating'. He said that she was 'scary'. Perhaps I needed to give him the benefit of the doubt.

I smiled at him. 'I'm sorry about your ankle and your . . . y'know.'

'S'OK. Seems like I didn't need to tell Shonna to lay off you anyway, because you can clearly do your own damage. Hell, I hear you totally stood up to her this morning,' said Tony.

'How do you know?' I asked.

'That girl – the blonde one. Glasses. Never stops talking . . .'

'Dena.' I should have known. Having Dena Barbulis in your class was like having your own dedicated outside broadcast unit.

'Look,' he said, smiling at me and clutching various bits of himself, 'I just don't want you to think I'm some sort of – I don't know – player or something. I'm not. I'm just me and I look out for my friends, and I don't want you or Billy to get hurt.'

It was ironic that Tony didn't want me to get hurt when I'd just smashed him up good and proper with a see-saw, and I started to laugh and then so did he. It felt pretty good – like a proper release of tension.

'OK?' he said.

'OK.'

Maybe he was a good guy after all. I had to believe it.

'Tell me something,' he said, 'because I just can't figure this out. Why were you and Shonna ever best friends?'

'It's complicated.' I said. Truthfully it was hard to remember.

'Because she is really, really mean. I mean, she is nasty. And you're so . . . you're so . . .'

What was I? Sweet? Cute? Tiny? Shy?

'You're so not like that.'

I fixed him with a stare. 'How do you know I'm not like that?' Maybe I was. He didn't know me.

'I just do. You're honest. You're open. You shared that stuff with me about your dad and I know it's very important to you. I haven't said a word to anyone about it. You can trust me.' He was doing the Tony Cruz nod again and I didn't really mind it just for a moment. 'You even told me not to laugh at Shonna the other day and I stopped!'

'Yeah, well, that was stoopid,' I said, 'I wouldn't say that now – not after the last few days.'

'That girl is devious. She's screwed up.'

'Aren't we all? Look at me – I'm surfing the net looking for my dad.'

'Did you get any leads from those files we found the other day? Billy won't tell me anything. He says it's all confidential.'

I liked that Billy was respecting my privacy.

'We're going to follow one of them up tomorrow. Number 278.'

'Quick work!' said Tony.

'You should get back to school – it's nearly lunchtime,' I said. 'The nurse'll fix you up. She did my lip the other day.'

'And I heard that wasn't an accident either,' said Tony. He stared up at me questioningly. I didn't say anything. I just shrugged. I could see the little scar above *his* top lip. I liked it.

'These are mean girls,' I said, 'but I don't think Shonna will try anything like that again, not after today.'

We were really close to each other and I noticed that a strand of Tony's hair had come out of place. It was such nice hair, really dark and wavy, and this stray bit was dangling down temptingly as he crouched on the ground rolling up his sock. I wondered if it was the sort of hair that would ping back if you pulled it. It looked so springy. I couldn't help it and my hand went out to touch it . . . but then he moved and stood up to his full height.

'Well, she can answer to me if she does,' he said, oblivious to what I'd been about to do. 'From what I heard, you've got her and her cronies running scared anyway.'

He walked me back to the flats and I turned to face him just outside the entrance because whatever else was or wasn't going on, I did think he'd been brave to come and see me like that. A little crazy, but brave. And I wanted to tell him so.

'Listen,' I said, 'thanks for coming here to talk to me.'

He shrugged.

'No, really. It was a bit of a shock to find you on the doorstep, but it's cleared the air and I do believe you. I think.'

'Cool,' said Tony, and he held his hand out. It was an odd gesture – I couldn't decide if he wanted me to hold it or shake it. So then, having conducted myself with so much self-control, I ruined it all. I did something very, very weird. I walked up to Tony Cruz and I kissed him very gently on the lips. It wasn't like a great big snog, just a warm, friendly kiss. And then I watched him walk off down the street. He was limping a bit.

OK, I just blurred the situation myself now, I thought.

21

Don't Get Me Wrong, I Do Love My Mum

When I got up to the flat, Mum was in, dammit. Why does she always turn up when I want the place to myself?

I could hear her as I put my key in the door. She was shouting.

'I rang the other day . . . Mrs Nathanson. N-A-T-H-A-N-S-O-N. I would like to speak to your manager, so just go and find him and don't put me on hol—'

She put our brand-new replacement phone on speaker as I came in. I wondered how long it would be until this one hit the wall. 'Greensleeves' was playing. I guessed it was the bank on the other end again. They always played that tune.

'Sweetheart,' she said, 'is everything OK? I had a call from school. So I came home and you weren't here.' Her hair was fluffed up at the front and she was pink in the face.

'Oh,' I said casually. 'That. They called you?' I wanted my lack of concern to cancel out Mum's anxiety. I didn't want any hassle.

'They said you walked out.'

'Well . . .'

She was looking at me kindly. It didn't seem like she was exactly angry.

'What happened? Did you have a row with someone? Was it Shonna?'

'Kind of.'

'We need to sort this, love,' said Mum. She pulled a chair out for me. 'We can't have you walking out of school upset and–'

'What do we need to sort?' I remained standing. I didn't want to sit down.

'Well.' Mum massaged her temples. 'Let's start with why you walked out of school.'

'I got my period,' I lied. 'I didn't have anything with me.'

'That isn't what the school told me.'

'Well, it's not the kind of thing you broadcast actually and anyway, if you know, then why are you asking me?'

We glared at each other. I was no longer being casual and I could see that Mum was losing patience.

'*Mrs Nathanson?*' 'Greensleeves' had stopped. Someone was on the speakerphone.

'Yes!' Mum shouted into the speaker, leafing through some bank statements as she did so and mouthing 'sorry' at me.

I shrugged and started to walk to my bedroom.

'Sadie!' Mum shouted and I jumped. 'Sadie, I am trying to be reasonable. Now, will you just wait, please? I haven't finished talking.'

'*I beg your pardon?*' said the man's voice on speakerphone.

'Not you.'

How is it that mums can yell at you and in the same breath tell you that they are being reasonable? I slumped down on the chair after all.

'Shouting at me isn't reasonable,' I said.

'Listen to me.' Mum was talking to the bank now, or whoever it was unfortunate enough to be on the other end of her call. 'Freezing my account is not reasonable either.'

Everything was about being reasonable today it seemed.

'It's fine, Mrs Nathanson,' said the man's voice. 'Your account seems to be in order as of ten o'clock this morning.'

'I paid a cheque in. The week before last. That's more than five working days ago – it should have cleared by now.'

'As I said, as of ten o'clock this morning your account is in order.'

'Good. Well then. Good. So why did your other man tell me it hadn't cleared and it was all still frozen?'

'My colleague must have been looking at an earlier screen.'

I stood up. I was sick of waiting for Mum to finish.

'Don't move a muscle,' said Mum. 'We need to talk.'

'We are talking,' said the man.

'Not you,' said Mum.

'Mrs Nathanson,' said the man, obviously trying to sound reasonable, 'perhaps you should call back at a more convenient time?'

Mum frowned. 'This is a convenient time. Well, it's as convenient a time as any.'

'*If you don't mind my saying so, it doesn't sound like it. It sounds as if you're having an argument with someone.*'

'It's my teenage daughter.'

'*Ah, well I sympathise. I have a thirteen-year-old.*'

'Mine is fifteen.'

'*Tell her to sit down and you'll deal with her when she's wiped the make-up off, turned the music down and come out of the bathroom.*'

It was just great. They went on like that for ten minutes with me sitting there apparently not allowed to move.

'Now listen to me,' said Mum, having sorted out her finances and finally turning to me with her full attention. 'I – *we* – have a duty of care. You cannot just walk out of school in the middle of a lesson and not tell anybody where you're going.'

'Shonna and Imelda were mean to me. I got into maths and found I'd come on, so I legged it.'

Mum ran her fingers through her hair. God, that style was like a crime against hairdressing. How could I have a mum with hair like that? Why wouldn't she let me loose on it?

She sighed. 'I am *really* sorry you're having such a

rotten time. It sounds like Shonna is behaving very badly. I know Jeanette's having problems with her, it's not just you. Just don't let her get the better of you.'

'Wha'ever, Mum.'

'Don't "wha'ever" your mother like that!' said the man on speakerphone, who was apparently still with us.

Mum switched him off. 'No, Sadie, don't "wha'ever" me, please. Maybe you need to talk to someone else though. I don't seem to be able to solve this stuff any more, do I? We always end up having a row. I suppose it's inevitable, but we used to be so close. I feel like you're keeping so much from me.'

For once she was right. I was keeping stuff from her. And that wasn't going to change any time soon.

Don't get me wrong. I do love my mum. She just has absolutely no clue about what goes on in my life these days.

Current Mood: stood up to meangirlz. kissed nodding boy

Groovechick2: congrats. U hav achieved level 50 combat rating & romance 2!

SayD: lying 2 mum about searching 4 dad - feel weird

Groovechick2: u need to connect wiv her

SayD: u sound like school counsellor

Groovechick2: guess where I spent half my life?

SayD: don't wanna tell her. Wanna do it myself. But don't wanna lie

Groovechick2: u can't hv it all SayD

22

Come In, Dad #241

Tuesday 2nd October

Hairstyle: Odango お団子 - Double or Triple Buns

This outrageous style was worn by Queen Serenity in the manga series *Sailor Moon*. Make a centre parting with a very thin comb. Using two elastics, make two high pigtails. Secure each one as a bun with hairpins. Brush one side of the remaining hair up, hiding the parting that was created by the buns, and tie it back. Now curl the ends and add ribbons or whatever you prefer. You *are* a manga queen!

OK. I'd gone from fierce ponytail girl to Queen Serenity in twenty-four hours. It was kind of a quirky look, but when I checked it out in the reflective library door at lunchtime, I was pleased with the result. Miss Frame seemed to like it too.

'Good hair, Sadie,' she said.

But I hadn't come to the library for compliments

and I hadn't come there to hide out. I hadn't heard a sausage from my apparently successfully delivered email to Dad #241, Abraham Smith. Dads #254 and 278 were in the pipeline, but what if Dad #241 was the one? I couldn't just let him go. I'd been waiting five days and now I needed to send another email.

From: Sadie.nat@cupcakedanceparty.com
Sent:Tues 2/10 12:26
To: abe.smith@kent.gov.uk
Subject: Hi Again

Dear Abraham Smith

I already sent you one email and there's no reply so I just thought I'd send you another one – just because, well, because I want to and Miss Frame who's this kooky teacher here says I should write like we're having a conversation. So anyway, I live in the city and I'm still at school and I live in this area called Hackney in East London. I was born here and I pretty much know everyone around about five roads, but if I go outside my 'zone', I don't recognise anyone. Plus I'm not allowed by my mum.

How about you? Do you travel much? I've been to the Isle of Wight with the school and I once went to an island called Borocay in the Philippines where my Uncle Zé's family live. The sea was so blue and my cousin Billy and I slept outside, and I remember the stars were like pretend stars – like someone had hung them up just above our heads because they were so bright.

It was beautiful there.

From
Sadie Nathanson

And then I went totally mad and I put my home address on there too. It wasn't sensible, I know, but I thought maybe Abraham Smith was as old as Mum and might feel more at home with envelopes and handwriting and stamps.

Miss Frame came over and leaned on the edge of the table again. She folded her arms very precisely.

'How's the email coming along, Sadie?' she asked.

'I sent it already.'

She raised her eyebrows. 'That's great.'

'He didn't reply to the first one, but it wasn't returned either so I thought I'd just send another one.'

Miss Frame stood there smiling at me. She did her breathing-in thing with her neat little chest going up and down – she was so . . . measured in everything she did. Like she weighed up every movement.

'Sadie,' she said eventually, 'did you have a fight with Shonna Matthews in class yesterday?'

I looked up at her. She took my breath away with her directness. She was looking straight at me, but she was smiling.

'Well . . .' I said.

I wasn't sure whether the truth would get me into more trouble. So far there had been no comeback from yesterday's scene in the maths room other than my bringing a letter in from home explaining my sudden absence – the version I'd given Mum anyhow. Jeanette Matthews hadn't even 'been up the school' in her usual hands-on-leopard-print-hips way. So I thought it best to remain non-committal about the whole thing.

'Well . . .' I said again.

The trouble is that teachers like Miss Frame don't

give up. They're like Terminator units – they just keep going.

'Sadie, has Shonna Matthews been bullying you?'

A direct question deserves a direct answer and I wanted to say 'yes', but then that wouldn't take account of *why* Shonna was being mean. It wouldn't take account of all that stuff with her dad and my dad, because deep down when I was being charitable, and Shonna and Imelda weren't kicking me or cussing me, I didn't really blame Shonna for all of it. In fact I felt a bit like some of it *was* my fault.

I stared blankly at Miss Frame, hoping she'd let it go, but I could see she wasn't going to.

'Yes,' I said finally. 'I stood up to her and yes, she's been bullying me.'

'Well, good for you!' said Miss Frame brightly and went back to her computer.

I watched her out of the corner of my eye, typing away with her neat little hands. Really, the woman was self-contained. You couldn't imagine her ever losing her cool.

She would never allow herself to be bullied.

23

The Bodyguard

Tony Cruz was waiting for me outside my English class that afternoon. He was leaning against the radiator, doing that eyes closed thing. All I could think was, *OMG I kissed you yesterday and now I have to go back to being normal with you, but in front of my entire class*.

His hair looked great too which didn't help in terms of the Total Boy Paralysis thing. He must've washed it, but I think he uses a diffuser because he really gets lift, unlike Billy who dries his way too flat. The stray strand in Tony's hair was hanging down again though. My fingers itched to touch it.

On the face of it, being met out of class by Tony Cruz was practically the coolest thing that had ever happened to me. But in reality it was like one of those nightmares where you're having a legendary day at school until you realise that you don't have your pants on, or the toilet is on the stage in the assembly hall and you're busting to go. Tony and I had an audience and I couldn't think of a single thing to say to him.

'Hi,' I said as thirty-one jerks stood in a row staring at us.

'Hi,' said Tony. 'Just keeping an eye on things. How's it going?'

'OK, I guess.'

'All quiet on the Western Front?'

'Sure.'

So he walked me to maths. Meanwhile I tried to think of a million different conversations, which all turned out to be more stupid than each other. How was it that yesterday, when I was pissed off with him, I could talk to Tony Cruz like a normal person, but today, when I liked him again, I could only come up with the dumbest lines? *What do you think of my Tuesday hair – am I Queen Serenity?* *What's your view on cryogenics?* *Do you have a dog?*

'Did you–' I started to say.

'Cool hair,' he said.

'Thanks.'

'See you later.'

Inside the maths room I looked over at Shonna. For

once she didn't turn and glare at me. She just looked at her notebook and scribbled down the equations from the whiteboard. She even put her hand up and answered a question. Incorrectly. Which was a bit of a relief.

At the end of maths, Tony was waiting again. *Eeek*, I thought, *it's a really long walk to the science block and I still can't think of anything to say and my entire class is still here staring at us and I kissed you yesterday.*

'You'd make a great bodyguard, y'know,' I said, and then instantly regretted it. Bodyguards: universally acknowledged to be muscle-bound thickos.

Tony shrugged at me and smiled. 'Thanks . . . I think,' he said.

'How's your ankle . . . and your *itlogs*?' I was thinking of him and the see-saw the day before.

'My what?'

'You know what. That's Uncle Zé speak.'

'Of course it is. By the way, what did you actually cuss at Shonna yesterday? I heard it was pretty strong!'

'Who told you?'

'I have my spies.'

'I called her something like a "Special hot dog with cheese fries, an iced coke and all in a sesame seed bun

I'm loving it, I'm loving it, I'm loving it". It sounds fierce if you're not from the Philippines.'

Tony started to laugh. 'I am lovin' it.'

I'd made him laugh. He thought I was funny.

'By the way, you don't have to do this, y'know,' I said.

'Do what?'

'This. This meeting me out of class thing.'

'I don't think I *need* to do this,' said Tony. 'You cussed Shonna good and proper yesterday morning – even if it turns out that you only called her a thick shake with a pickled onion. But yesterday I did say she'd have to answer to me, didn't I? I just needed to check in with you and I wanted you to trust what I said.'

'And I do.'

'And I like to keep my word.'

'Shonna hasn't even looked at me all morning.'

'She's probably scared you're going to ask her if she wants fries with that, madam.'

'To be honest,' I said, because I wanted to try and be straight with Tony Cruz and not blur things or talk quietly so that he had to lean forward or any stupid trick like that, 'I can't think of anything to say to you

201

when you're walking me between lessons because school is so dumb that there's just nothing to say about it – is there?'

'I guess not.'

'Plus they're all staring at us because they have nothing else to do and *Good as it Gets* isn't on TV until tonight so they've nothing to talk about.'

He shrugged at me and did the Tony Cruz nod – which was very reassuring.

'I'll see you later then?' I said.

'Later,' he said, 'and good luck for tonight.'

I looked blank for a second before I remembered that I had an appointment to have my buttocks liposuctioned that very evening. When the bell went at three, Billy and I would be running off to find Dad #278.

24

The Thing is . . . Sperm Donation

Billy and I spotted what we took to be Dr Swain-Coles getting out of an oversized black taxi by his clinic in Harley Street. We were some distance away, but even from there he looked just as he had on his website photo, with dark hair and smartly dressed in a dark suit. A glamorous-looking woman came down the steps from his clinic.

'Oh hello, Dr Swain-Coles!' she said. This was further confirmation.

The woman was abnormally tall. She seemed to tower over him.

'Is that taxi larger than usual?' I said.

'No,' said Billy.

'That woman is unusually tall though, right?'

'No,' said Billy again. 'Dr Swain-Coles is very short.'

'He looked tall in the photo,' I said.

'He was sitting down.'

'Well, he had a tall sitting-down look going on. But I guess short would be about right really,' I said. 'I'm not exactly on the basketball squad.'

So we went into Dr Swain-Coles's cosmetic surgery clinic and, as we went up the steps, I wondered whether, by the time we came back down the steps, I would finally know who my dad was. It was an odd thought. Not the sort of thought you have every day. I had been feeling fairly calm right up until that point, but with each step butterflies began to swarm in my stomach until I felt so nervous that I almost suggested turning round and going home again. Billy was in front of me and something about the rigid set of his shoulders and the determination of his walk kept me glued to my mission.

The building was one of those solid, flat-fronted London houses like you see on costume dramas. Then we stepped over the threshold from the hectic street and into a soft, peaceful world of palest peach and magnolia, plush sofas and a thick cream carpet. Calming music was playing in the background, like it had on the website, and the receptionist who greeted us had the widest smile I'd ever seen. She was like an ad for teeth bleaching. Maybe she got a staff discount.

'My name's Sadie Nathanson,' I said to the receptionist. 'I have an appointment.'

My voice didn't sound quite like my own voice. It was louder and lower than usual. I felt like I was on a stage pretending to be serious and grown-up.

'Oh yes!' said the receptionist. She looked down at her grand old-fashioned appointments book and then she smiled again – the sort of warm smile which might reassure people about to have things sucked out of or pumped into their bodies. I idly wondered where they put the things they sucked out or pumped in. I mean, was there a holding bay for 'Body Fat in Waiting' somewhere? OMG. *Yeuch*.

'Sadie Nathanson,' said the receptionist, and she gestured to my name in her appointments book with a set of amazing purple manicured nails glittering with rhinestones. 'Do take a seat.'

Billy and I sat down obediently, sinking into velvety, butterscotch-coloured chairs. It was like sitting in Angel Delight.

We'd changed out of our school uniforms. We'd caught the bus. We'd found the clinic. We had an appointment. Now we just had to see the doctor to find out if he was my dad. Obviously that was going to be the hardest bit.

I was now so nervous that I only vaguely glanced around the waiting room before focusing in on a magazine in front of me called *Country Homes and Gardens*. I'd been rather dreading seeing people swathed in bandages with terrible scars, but the young woman with her teenage daughter and the smiley man opposite looked pretty much on the normal side to me.

Then I looked a bit closer. The woman with the teenage daughter had the smoothest skin imaginable, except her eyes were really wide apart. They seemed to sit at either side of her head, like a rabbit, which was kind of weird, but it was her neck that completely gave her away as it was more wrinkled than Aunty Rita's. It was quite possible that she was the girl's grandmother.

The man opposite was vaguely smiling, but after a while I realised that this was because his face was rigidly stuck in that position. He could well have been furious, but you just wouldn't know.

I took a deep breath in and looked around the room. I didn't want to be caught staring. On the opposite wall

hung an enormous photograph of Dr Swain-Coles —
smiling over his waiting patients. I studied it carefully
and tried to compare his face to my own. His brow
didn't crinkle when he smiled, but perhaps he'd Botoxed
himself. It was impossible to see his eyes properly as
they were distorted behind what looked like rather
thick glasses. I, on the other hand, have 20/20 vision.
His hair was dark, like my own, as were his eyebrows.
Aside from this there was nothing to suggest that I
shared half his genes. He looked like what he was. A
total stranger.

I was so deep in thought that Billy had to nudge me
to tell me my name had been called. It was our turn to
go in to see the doctor.

I took a deep breath. This was potentially 'it'. And
there was no going back now. My gut began a rapid
spin cycle.

Dr Swain-Coles was seated behind the most enormous
desk I had ever seen. The office was large, but the desk
seemed to take up most of it. His chair was clearly at its
highest setting and his feet were definitely resting on a
box because, like his photo, Dr Swain-Coles did look

tall. And we knew that he wasn't. On his desk were several silver-framed photographs, which you might have expected to be of his wife or children, but turned out to be of different cats – I could just catch small glimpses of tails and whiskers as Billy and I walked in and stood on the opposite side of the enormous desk.

Dr Swain-Coles didn't look at us. He just said, 'Take a seat why don't you,' and looked down at a notepad then up at a computer screen. When he eventually looked straight ahead, he did a bit of a double take.

'Sadie Nathanson?' he said questioningly.

'That's me,' I said, the words half-catching in my throat which felt dry like dead leaves. I was aware of a clock ticking loudly in the office. There was an odd metallic taste in my mouth and my tongue was like an old sock.

There was a jug of water on the table in front of me so I poured a glass and took a swig.

'And you are how old?' said Dr Swain-Coles.

'I'm eighteen,' I lied, 'but . . .'

'If you don't mind my saying so,' said Dr Swain-Coles gently, 'you are a little on the *young* side for this clinic. I know you filled a lot of details in on the registration form, but in my experience young girls only ever come to see me about one thing: breast augmentation. Am I right?'

He didn't wait for me to reply. 'You really should be here with your mother, dear, not your . . .' he eyed Billy, 'your boyfriend.'

It was like being told off by a kindly teacher and even though I knew I *wasn't* actually interested in having cosmetic surgery, in that instant I felt that I *was* and furthermore that I *should* have brought my mother with me. I opened my mouth, but the words simply weren't coming out. Billy stared at me, willing me to say something. I downed more water.

Dr Swain-Coles came out from behind his desk, which was a surprise all over again because I'd forgotten he was so much shorter than I'd thought. He looked as if he was coming out on his knees. Really, if we hadn't seen him getting out of the cab earlier, the shock might have finished me off.

'So tell me what you feel is . . . *problematic* in your appearance, Miss . . .'

'Nathanson.'

'Nathanson, that's it. You're still a young girl – you

won't really have grown into yourself yet.'

He strode over to a large wooden cabinet in the corner of his office, still not giving me a chance to reply, even if I could.

'I always show something to the young girls who come here wanting the same operation as you, dear.'

He opened a drawer and took something out of a plastic bag. 'Here! Catch!' he said, and threw it to me.

Luckily my reflexes aren't bad because I was able to catch the thing he had thrown. I wasn't quite sure how lucky I was when I surveyed what landed in my hand. It was squashy and cool to the touch. It seemed to be clear liquid in a plastic pouch.

'And another!' said Dr Swain-Coles, this time throwing a pouch to Billy, who duly caught it and raised his eyebrows questioningly at me.

'Those,' said Dr Swain-Coles walking towards us, 'are breast implants.'

'Huh?' I said.

Billy nearly dropped his.

'Feel the weight of them,' said Dr Swain-Coles, 'and imagine having to carry those around for the rest of your life. Food for thought, eh? Second thoughts, eh?'

I knew I had to speak. I knew I had to tell Dr Swain-Coles why we'd really come to see him. I dug my fingernails into my hands, trying to force the words out.

And then Billy spoke. 'Actually,' he said, 'that's not why we're here at all.'

Somehow his speaking for me helped to get me going again.

'Dr Swain-Coles!' I burst out, finally finding my voice. 'I didn't come to see you about a boob job!' I was so nervous that I pretended for a moment that I was Miss Frame, and I placed my hands very deliberately by my sides, mainly to stop them from shaking. I was still holding the plastic breast and it was wibbling and wobbling in my fingers.

Dr Swain-Coles retreated behind his desk immediately like it was some kind of safety barrier.

'What do you mean, you didn't come here about a boob job?' he said. 'I'm not quite sure I catch your drift.'

I wondered if he was about to press a panic button.

'Well,' I said, and I took a deep breath in again, just like Miss Frame. I watched my chest rise and fall and then I said, 'The thing is . . . sperm donation.'

It wasn't what I'd planned to say. It wasn't exactly

the speech I'd practised with Billy on the journey over.

Dr Swain-Coles paused. He sat down, transforming once more into his tall self, and smiled at me. 'I'm afraid we don't do IVF here. That's a very different sort of a clinic. No shortage of places nearby, mind you. Again, Miss Nathanson, you seem awfully young to be enquiring . . .'

'What she means is—' said Billy.

'What I mean is,' I interrupted, 'sixteen years ago I think my mum might have got your sperm off the Internet – off a website where they put you in touch with sperm donors.'

I peered at Dr Swain-Coles to see if there was any look of recognition, but he was staring down with great concentration at his blank notepad.

I went on. 'You see, I found an email with your details and I wondered . . .'

Dr Swain-Coles looked up and stared straight into my eyes. His own seemed to be glistening behind his glasses.

'I wondered . . .' I couldn't go on. My throat was dry again.

'She wondered if you were her dad,' said Billy.

There was a very long pause.

'Good gracious,' said Dr Swain-Coles eventually, and then he smiled at me. 'Well, I wasn't expecting that this afternoon. Nip and tuck, yes! Are you my dad? Good grief! Now that's what I call a bit of a curve ball!' And he sat there blinking and smiling.

And smiling and blinking.

And when he'd finished blinking, he did a bit more smiling.

And when he was through with smiling, he did some more blinking.

Impatience rose up in my throat. I'd stated my mission. Why was he stalling?

'I just want to know . . . I just want to *know*, you see.' My voice was getting higher now because I'd asked him the question and I wanted him to tell me the answer, and he was just sitting there smiling and blinking at me like a — like a demented owl. 'I just want to find out who my dad is. I found a clue and now I've started and I can't stop!'

'Yes, yes,' said Dr Swain-Coles calmly, 'I see that. I do see that.'

There was a silence which seemed to go on forever

– like when they're counting up the votes on *Good As it Gets* and they want the audience at home to be bouncing off the walls with anticipation. And then Dr Swain-Coles spoke.

'The thing is . . . Have you heard of Tay-Sachs?'

Oh, not another diversion. Was he going to throw something else to us now? A fake buttock? A couple of pecs perhaps?

Billy shook his head. 'No,' he said.

'It's a disease,' said Dr Swain-Coles. 'It's carried in the genes – on chromosome 15 to be precise.'

'Oh,' I said.

'I'm a carrier,' said Dr Swain-Coles. 'I don't have the disease, but I carry it.'

He stood up, came out from behind his desk and held his hand out to Billy.

'Breast?' he said.

Billy looked confused, then handed over the implant that he'd somehow put in his back pocket.

I handed mine over without the prompt. I was glad to be shot of it. I just wanted Dr Swain-Coles to get on with what he was saying, but he didn't seem to be in any hurry. He replaced the breasts carefully in the bag and shut the door of the cabinet, then turned back to us.

'No, Sadie,' he said. 'I'm not who you're looking for.'

My heart skipped a beat. My breath caught in my throat. Finally I had an answer.

He went on. 'She didn't take my contribution. Your mother. No one did, because when I was tested it turned out that I was a carrier of Tay-Sachs. Defective genes. No symptoms – no one in my family ever had it. But I carry the gene. If I had a baby with another carrier there's a strong chance that it would be passed on to the child. It's a terrible disease. Not survivable.'

'Oh,' I said.

'So I can't be your dad, you see, Sadie – Miss Nathanson. In fact,' his eyes were glistening again, 'I'm not anyone's dad – so there we are!'

'Oh,' I said again.

He wasn't my dad and in that instant the excitement that had been running through my body just ebbed right away.

'We thought–' said Billy.

'Sadly no,' said Dr Swain-Coles. 'I can't help you. Would *love* to, but can't.'

215

We stood up because that seemed the natural thing to do.

'Now I must attend to my next patient,' said Dr Swain-Coles. 'I wish you good luck on your quest,' and he came forward and shook my hand and Billy's.

'You know,' he said to both of us in general, but really to no one in particular, 'there are people who choose to donate for purely altruistic reasons. I really did want to make a difference to people's lives.' He stared right at me again with his shiny eyes. 'I'm glad your mother found another donor. I do hope you manage to track him down.'

And then we were out in the corridor and I don't really remember how we got through the waiting room because it's hard to see when your eyes are full of tears. Next thing we were coming down the steps of the building and it had turned out that Dr Swain-Coles wasn't my dad after all. But you know what? He was a really nice guy.

Groovechick2's Current Mood: I wanna b free

SayD: I wann b xpensiv

Groovechick2: ha ha. How ur day? Mine full of xams

SayD: U wouldn't believe mine if I told u – Scary. Exciting. Sad

Groovechick2: y sad?

SayD: bcos u no I'm lookin for my dad? and this guy seemed nice but turned out not 2b dad after all

Groovechick2: that's hard. Wot a let down

SayD: made me feel really empty inside. is that weird? I don't even no him

Groovechick2: maybe . . .

SayD: there's this teacher at skool & she's really calm all the time & she duz this calm breathing thing & she's careful abt everything & u can't tell wot she's thinking & she keeps it all to herself instead of making a big fuss like my whole family duz about nothing

Groovechick2: u wanna b her?

SayD: is that weird 2?

Groovechick2: bet she's a case outside of skool – bet u she's a loony

25

Friendship is Never About Accessories

Wednesday 3rd October

Hairstyle: French Twist

This is the ultimate elegant hairstyle, elongating the neck and giving you a sleek profile. All you need is a comb and hairgrips. Pull your hair back into a ponytail, twist the hair from the base and pin. You will have the poise of Audrey Hepburn. Enjoy your very own *Breakfast at Tiffany's!*

It was eerie how quiet Shonna had become these days. It was two days since our fight and there hadn't been a peep out of her. Take Wednesday afternoon for instance. During class she just sat and did her work. When she was asked to read out her assignment, she read it out. Without making any cracks or going, 'What me, Miss? You want me to read? But it's boring, Miss. I might fall asleep.'

218

But the weirdest thing of all was that she left me alone. We still sat together in business studies. Imelda was in a different group and there weren't enough tables to be able to sit on your own and be all mean and moody and stare out of the window like you hated everyone. So Shonna and I had to share a desk. Usually it was horrendous because she'd try to sit as far away from me as possible. She'd squeeze on to her side of the desk and put her pencil case down the middle like a barrier, and if anything of mine – like my shoe or my paper or my book – even so much as brushed her, she'd tut at me under her breath. Although she'd do it so everyone else could hear. And if I ever answered a question (which I tried hard not to, although business is one of my most favourite subjects, next to design) she'd mutter 'teacher's pet' under her breath or 'girlie swot'.

But this particular afternoon she was totally and utterly silent. Sullen. I tried not to look at her, but every time I did she had a face on her like a melted welly. Evidently that look was no longer reserved exclusively for me. I'd seen it used on all the teachers and most of the students. Maybe it wasn't just about me any more. Maybe she hated everyone.

At end-of-school I could see Tony Cruz talking to Kip and some of the other guys on the football team outside the school gate. They were high-fiving and low-fiving all over the place. Boys were so weird like that – the way they bonded. They needed an excuse – a sport or an accessory – to connect them. Sometimes I wondered just how Billy and Tony were ever friends. I mean, where does a geek meet a jock (albeit a jock who's a secret geek)? The answer was simple – another accessory. They bonded over a guitar and a computer, and Billy's haircut sealed it.

With girls, friendship is *never* about accessories. But what *was* it about? Shonna and I had been friends because we knew everything about each other. We knew what our children's names would be and where we kept our spare keys and that neither of us had a dad exactly. We were friends because we knew that we would be friends forever and ever. Until the day Shonna decided to 'out' me in human biology and I realised that we simply *weren't* friends any more.

I went to walk by the football boys at the gate. I pretended not to see Tony clocking me and carried right on by and . . .

'You all right then, Sadie?' said Tony.

He was suddenly beside me and starting to walk in step with me, which was odd because he lived in the opposite direction.

'I'm OK,' I said. 'You don't usually go this way round.'

'I'm nipping over to Billy's – mind if I walk with you?'

'Not really.'

In fact, it was just perfect because thirty-one people weren't watching us and I could think of plenty to say this time. It was my moment to be totally natural with Tony Cruz – just like Groovechick2 had suggested. Maybe, just maybe, he really liked *me*.

'Listen,' he said in his confiding way, 'are you going to come to our gig Friday night? We're playing at The Forge.'

I'd heard about it from Billy – it was some kid's sixteenth birthday party – but I hadn't really paid it much attention. Now I was listening hard because I thought Tony might be asking me to go to it. Like really *asking* me for real – *on a date*.

'I'm not invited to the party or anything,' I said, 'and

I don't even know the boy that's having it.'

'Well, I'm inviting you,' Tony said. He said it very definitely. Like there could be no arguing with it. Maybe he'd actually enjoyed that kiss the other day. Clearly it hadn't scared him. But was it actually a date? Did it qualify?

'Sure,' I said. 'Well, that sounds good then.'

He looked a bit sheepish for a moment and then he said, 'Sadie, I've got something to ask you. It's important.'

Oh my God – was this it? Was he really asking me on a date now?

'Sure, what is it?' I said, trying to keep my heart from leaping out of my chest at him.

'I wondered if you might, like, style us? Rock Dove, I mean.'

'Style you?'

'You know – make us look good. Hair and all that.'

Tony Cruz wasn't asking me out, but he was asking me to 'style' his band. OK. OK. I had to keep my head here. On a personal level this was totally the wrong question dammit, although it undeniably had potential. But in terms of business this was a very good opportunity.

Maybe my real future was about to start. In World of Warcraft terms I'd just been given my 'quest'. It was up to me to take it to the next level.

'Sure,' I said, 'I'll style you. I have tea at Billy's on Fridays, so it'll have to be after that.'

'It's a date then.'

It's a 'date'? There he went – blurring the lines again.

We walked on by the park towards Billy's. I thought of the last time we'd been in the playground, about that stray piece of Tony's hair and how I'd kissed him.

'How was Shonna today?' said Tony.

'You know what?' I said. 'She is really, really quiet.'

'She didn't start anything?'

'Not a peep. She never said a word all day. Usually she's at me every lesson, making my life a misery, but since Monday . . .'

'Since you called her a *filet-o'-fish* . . .'

'Well, yeah, since then – nothing. All quiet.'

We were outside Aunt Lilah's shop now. I turned to go.

'So will you come to the party?' he asked, putting his hand on my arm.

'Friday night, sure,' I said, trying to ignore the sparks

of electricity travelling up my arm. 'If I can make it through tomorrow.'

'What's happening?'

'Dad number 254.'

'Woah, heavy,' he said, and leaned against Aunt Lilah's shop window. My stomach dipped like I was on a rollercoaster.

'D'you want company – when you go and meet him?' he said. 'I mean, I know Billy'll be there and everything, but it might be intense and stuff.'

He was offering to come. He *must* like me. He *must*. But tomorrow was the wrong gig – the Dad-gig. I didn't really want him there. Dad #278 had been messy, and I didn't want Tony to see me messy. I wanted him to think of me as elegant, with poise, like the French Twist hairdo.

'It's OK,' I said. 'Like you say, Billy'll be there.'

'But you'll come to the party.'

'Sure.'

'It'll be a good night. I guarantee to deliver one good night.' He smiled at me.

'Smoooooth operator,' said a voice from high above. We both looked up to see Uncle Zé staring down from the lounge above the salon. He sounded cheerful, but he was doing the Teenage Boy Hostility Frown.

'Hi, Uncle,' I said. I decided to counter the hostility with extra bright and breeziness. 'I'm just going home.'

'Say hi to your ma, *anak*!' Uncle Zé called down to me.

'See you,' said Tony to me.

I walked down the street then turned and watched the back of Tony's neck as he went into the shop. I do really fancy the back of his neck.

I'd almost reached the corner by the minimarket when I heard Uncle Zé shouting. I stopped and turned round. He was right behind me. Red in the face from calling and running.

'*Ay naku*, you're deaf!' said Uncle. 'I'm glad I caught you, because we need to have a chat about something.'

This was going to be about Tony. I knew it. This was going to be about my standing next to Tony.

'Oh, ok,' I said. Uncle Zé and I had always got on pretty well, but this anti-boy-thing of his was definitely coming between us.

'Come on,' he said, taking my hand like I was a little kid again and leading me back along the road he'd just run along.

There are two doors outside my aunt's shop. If you choose the left-hand door, you enter the salon; if you choose the right-hand door, you find yourself in Café Zé. It's a daytime café that starts early and finishes early, so by three o'clock he's all sold out and cleaned up and at a loose end. When we were little kids it meant that he could pick us up from school and take us to the playground, but I don't know what Uncle Zé does when he's finished locking the café these days.

Now he was opening its green front door and letting me inside. Uncle's café is not much to look at with its faded bamboo patterned wallpaper, shabby cork floor, grey Formica tables and dog-eared travel posters of the Philippines tacked to the wall, but it smells delicious. It's garlic and rice and sweet, sweet marinated chicken or pork. That smell will always be home to me, and presumably to his customers, because Uncle's café is always busy.

He pulled a chair out for me at one of the tables. Then he went to the fridge behind the counter, took out two Cokes and something in a Tupperware, which he proceeded to heat up in the microwave. He placed it in front of me, steaming in a small white bowl with chopsticks.

'*Sinigang,*' he said solemnly, 'with chicken.'

He didn't ever need to tell me what he'd cooked because it was always completely yummy. I loved my uncle's cooking. Everyone did.

'Now eat that while I talk,' he said.

'OK,' I said. There was no escape.

'You like Tony Cruz,' said Uncle Zé.

I mumbled something about him being 'OK I guess,' but Uncle held up his hand to silence me.

'It wasn't a question,' he said, 'it was a statement of fact. You like Tony.'

I blushed. I couldn't help it.

Then he shrugged. 'We all like Tony! Billy, Lilah, even I like Tony.'

Then he ran through an endless list of all the other people in E9 who liked Tony. Even Zé's cousin Moss liked Tony apparently, and he didn't like anyone much since his divorce.

'Tony is Billy's friend,' continued Uncle.

He'd lost me a bit now. What was he getting at? Seemed to be skirting the 'issue' by stating the bleeding obvious.

'He's a good guy. He's not like that Shonna. Your

227

mother says she's gone bad. Even when she was a little girl, she was rude. And she never liked my food, which is worse. But Tony, he's a good boy. We like him. But . . .' Uncle Zé took a slurp of coke here and raised his finger in the air, 'he is a boy and he is seventeen years old.'

'*Nearly* seventeen,' I corrected him.

'Eat,' commanded Uncle. 'I'll talk.'

I peered down into my *Sinigang*, trying not to squirm as I waited for Uncle Zé to embark on the 'boys are only after one thing' talk.

'The point is,' said Uncle, 'you don't have your father to warn you about nearly seventeen-year-old boys. You know – the father with the shotgun guarding his daughter's bedroom, all of that.' He smiled at me. 'It's so old-fashioned of course. But you do have your Uncle Zé, and I'm saying that Tony is a sixteen-year-old boy and you need to just remember that. That's all.'

'I know,' I managed to say, in between mouthfuls of chicken. 'I know and I know.'

'Yes,' said Uncle, 'but knowing up here' (he tapped his temple) 'in this café with me and the *Sinigang*, and knowing what that really means, are different things.'

'Yes,' I said, 'I do see.'

'You need to be careful. You need to take care – even with Tony.'

Uncle Zé went over to the café window. 'I look out at this street, day and night, night and day. And what I see is *terrifying*.'

For a moment I wondered what Uncle could possibly be seeing in the street.

'Life! I see life! The young girls just like you, walking along the street, shrieking with their girlfriends one minute, and the next time you see them they're pushing a pram.'

'Really? The next time?' Honestly – what planet was Uncle on?

'Don't be cheeky, Sadie. You need to take care.'

'*Tito*, if there's one thing I know about it's how babies are made!'

I mean, seriously, when I first asked my mum 'where did I come from?' I got a whole different answer to 'Well, your dad worked in Accounts and we used to get the same bus . . .'

Uncle said nothing. He came and sat down.

'I do know, *tito*. Really. Please don't worry.' Perhaps if I looked serious enough, he would stop.

'No, but you don't know, *anak*. You don't know. You know right now, but six months down the line you might forget and you might think – what the hell! And you'll relax and–'

'*Tito*, I won't relax because you will be under the bed with a shotgun.'

Uncle's face clouded. He was failing to make his point.

'Tony is a good kid, don't get me wrong, but I saw you with him this afternoon, and at first I could only see him and I couldn't see who he was with and I thought, my God – it's a girl he's trying to impress, and then – it's my niece!'

My bowl was empty. I was hoping that might be the cue to be released from the conversation.

'I was surprised, but I was also concerned and I mentioned it to Lilah as I came through the shop just now–'

'You told Aunt Lilah? Oh God – was that really necessary?'

'Yes, I told your Aunt that you walked home with Tony. You know what she said?'

'D'you mean *said* or *yelled*?'

230

'Your Aunt Lilah is pretty laid back about it all compared to me. She says, "Zé, I've been a fifteen-year-old girl – it's not so bad. You are not so naive as you might think at that age."'

This sounded remarkably sensible for my Aunt Lilah. I didn't buy it at all. I was quite sure that she'd already called Mum and Great Aunty Rita to tell them that Uncle Zé had dragged me away half naked from Tony by my hair.

'So you see,' said my uncle, 'it's me that's making the fuss here – your silly old uncle, not your Aunt Lilah.'

'You're not silly,' I said because I genuinely did love my uncle and he did make the tastiest chook in E9.

'I am silly,' said Uncle, 'but I worry about both you and Billy. That's all. Now . . .' he picked up my bowl and took it behind the counter, 'you can go home.'

I breathed a sigh of relief. Lecture over. I tucked my chair back under the table and Uncle stood up and hugged me.

'I bet you're really glad you don't have a dad,' said Uncle, 'because one is enough, huh?'

'Yes. I guess,' I said.

It was only when I was walking back to the corner that I mulled over that line again. It was something Uncle had said to me a million times before and I'd never even thought twice about it. Until now.

Billy and I had an appointment to meet Dad #254 the next night. But was there really any point? Because I was beginning to wonder if I was barking up the wrong tree altogether, although that was something I wasn't nearly ready to think about . . .

Current Mood: My uncle just gave me a talk on the facts of life. eek

Groovechick2: OK, dish
SayD: my unc jus did his dad-bit. He polished his shotgun
Groovechick2: nightmare – how's search going?
SayD: abt to meet next 1. Nervous
Groovechick2: what u nervous abt?
SayD: what if he's a let-down. What if I don't like him?
Groovechick2: walk away. U can always walk away
SayD: can I tho? feel like I've come this far. I need to no. I can't walk away. Even if the next 1 is horrible. I've still got to no

26

Dad #254

Thursday 4th October

Hairstyle: The Farrah Fawcett

Seems like every era makes its own version of the style made famous by Farrah Fawcett. To be authentic you could use a 1970s curling wand, but for ease just apply mousse or gel to wet hair. Blow your hair dry upside down for fullness. Use straighteners on the root to flip the hair without curling. Pull the straighteners upward, creating a 'bend' in the hair. This is your 'flip'. Finish your Farrah with hairspray to keep the shape. Go, Charlie's Angel!

I switched on my old mobile as Billy and I arrived in central London and walked towards the Equity offices. It sprang into life and I noticed that there had been two calls. Two voicemails. When I listened in, the first message was someone shouting so loudly that I nearly dropped the phone. I went to the next message and it was the same. A man shouting. This time I could make out a few of the words — something about legal action. I passed the phone to Billy.

'Wow!' he said. 'I have no idea what he's saying, but he sounds really angry.'

'Maybe we should abandon ship,' I said. My palms were starting to feel distinctly sweaty and there was a definite tremor in my hands. I was nervous anyway, but the fact that Charles Ward sounded so incredibly hostile to our meeting wasn't helpful.

'Look,' said Billy, 'we're here now, Sadie. He can always not turn up if he's that against it. He does have that option.'

He was right. We were actually coming up to the building now. One part of me hoped that Charles Ward just wouldn't come, but there was another part of me — the braver bit — which hoped against all hope that he would. Just so I could know.

There were two men standing outside the Equity offices at the appointed time. Harry 'The Hurricane' Hodder was one of them. Definitely. Undeniably. It was him. We stood across the street and stared furtively at him.

'Look who it is,' hissed Billy in my ear. 'It's that smug idiot off the telly – the one Mum likes.'

'What's he doing here?' I said. 'D'you think the other man is Charles Ward?'

The other man was short and stout and wearing a hat. It was difficult to see what he looked like from the other side of the road. I wondered if the short man was Dad #254. I didn't feel like crossing over and approaching anyone just yet, so I pulled Billy back round the corner and out of sight.

Then my old phone vibrated. After a moment, I answered it, holding the phone away from my ear in case there was more shouting.

'Charles Ward here,' said an abrupt voice on the other end of the phone before I'd even managed 'Hello'.

My stomach went into its ultra-spin cycle, the one reserved specifically for meeting Dads.

'Hello,' I said as calmly as I could, 'this is Sadie Nathanson.'

Billy's eyes widened expectantly. I nodded at him and then grabbed the bottle of water he was holding and drank. My throat was a pile of dead leaves again.

'We had an appointment,' said Charles Ward.

'We did,' I agreed.

'Well, I'm here,' said Charles Ward. 'Where the hell are you?'

Oh dear. I wasn't entirely sure that I was ready for Rude Dad.

'I'm here too,' I said, peering round the corner and over the road at the two men – I was trying to see if Hat Man was on the phone. 'Excuse me, but are you wearing a hat?'

Billy poked me. He was waving at me and gesturing towards The Hurricane and Hat Man. It was some kind of manic semaphore. I had no idea what it meant.

'It's him! It's him!' he was stage-whisper-yelling.

Charles Ward continued furiously on the phone. 'No, I am not wearing a hat, but I warn you that my solicitor is.'

'Your solicitor?' I said.

Billy gave up miming and grabbed my arm. We crossed the street.

'I've got my solicitor here,' continued Charles Ward into my ear, 'so anything your measly rag cares to print we'll sue you for every penn–'

We were right outside the Equity offices approaching

237

the two men. Harry 'The Hurricane' Hodder was on his mobile. He tailed off. He peered right at me. I peered back. He started to laugh.

'But you're kids!' he said. 'Ha! Ha! Very good!'

He nudged the man in the hat and they both laughed. It was sort of fake laughing though. I stared at them. I was completely mystified as to what was going on. Why was the Hurricane laughing at us? What did any of this have to do with him?

Billy had a grasp on the situation even if I didn't.

'Actually,' he said, 'we're not kids. I'm nearly seventeen.'

I could see that my cousin adding an extra year to his age was pointless. We clearly still looked like kids to The Hurricane.

'Ha!' he said again. Then he turned away and spoke to Hat Man. 'Go and wait in the car. I can handle this. No sense making a scene!'

'What's going on?' I whispered to Billy, tugging at his sleeve. He was staring at The Hurricane.

'*Dad 254*,' he mouthed at me.

'You're not trying to get a scoop for your school paper, are you?' The Hurricane said, turning back towards us, 'because you should know that I always, *always* accommodate kids. I'm happy to do an interview. You don't need to blackmail me by dredging up embarrassing stories from my foolish past, y'know.'

'I don't understand,' I said. 'We're supposed to be meeting Charles Ward.'

The Hurricane raised an eyebrow. 'Look, sweetheart,' he said, 'you don't have to play dumb with me – you know I *am* Charles Ward. That's my real name. Harry Hodder is my Equity name. It's my stage name, though I don't know why I'm bothering to explain this to you – you know it already. Well done for finding it out though. Top marks.'

'But we didn't,' said Billy. 'We didn't know.'

'No, we didn't,' I said. I was shaking my head in agreement, but my mind was racing to catch up with the situation: my dad? Harry 'The Hurricane' Hodder? The rudest celeb on telly? MY DAD? Aunt Lilah would be ecstatic. And yet it seemed so unlikely.

For a moment I tried to look at him in a detached way, as if I'd never ever seen him before. His hair had an auburn tinge and his skin was lightly freckled – you didn't notice any of that on the telly. There was not one

239

single feature I could pick out that corresponded to mine. He was very tall and his hands and feet were positively enormous. I looked down at my stubby fingers. It did not compute. Any of it. Until his expression changed. And then I saw it – undeniably – a deep groove in the centre of his forehead. A worry crinkle. The man had a worry crinkle. Just like mine.

'How did you find out about this?' The Hurricane continued. He'd got my letter out of his pocket now, and he waved it at me. 'I guess we all do crazy things in our youth, don't we? I *think*, if I remember rightly, that when I signed up for the website, I wanted to do some good in the world. I never got paid for it. You can put *that* in your article.'

He said this and prodded my schoolbag for emphasis – as if he expected me to start taking notes in my junior reporter's notepad. I became aware that people walking by were staring at us. Nudging each other and pointing at The Hurricane.

'And,' The Hurricane continued, oblivious, 'you might also want to put something in about the amount of charity work I do. That never makes the papers, does it?'

I needed him to stop talking. I had to tell him that this was about Charles Ward and not about Harry Hodder. I wanted to say this was about real life, not television.

An elderly lady in a plastic rain bonnet stopped dead in front of us. 'Are you off the telly?' she asked The Hurricane.

'Yes, madam, I am,' he said and beamed. Actually, it was more of a smirk.

'You're that newsreader, aren't you? The one who fought cancer.'

'No,' said the Hurricane. He was no longer smirking.

'Oh go on, you are – the one with the growths,' she insisted, nudging him with her bony elbow in an overfamiliar way. 'I've a memory for faces.'

'No, you have me confused,' said The Hurricane.

'Well, you're a dead ringer,' said the old lady. 'Not as good-looking though, and you've got hips. It's those trousers. I don't like a man with hips. I don't trust 'em.'

I caught Billy's eye and in spite of our utter bewilderment we both sniggered.

The Hurricane abruptly turned his back on the woman and faced me and Billy. 'So tell me,' he said, 'how did you find out about my "good gift"?'

Billy and I looked blank.

Behind us we could hear the woman muttering, 'Men with hips – don't like 'em,' as she toddled off down the street.

'No, really,' The Hurricane continued, 'I don't think anyone's ever asked me about it before. They've dug up everything else under the sun – girlfriends, wives, drugs, surgery – you name it! But never this.'

Billy looked at me pleadingly – he wanted me to say something. Anything. I didn't know whether to leave right now and risk never knowing if Charles Ward/ Harry Hodder was my donor, or I could stay and get a straight answer. The trouble was that the situation was so bizarre, so utterly unexpected, all I could do was open and shut my mouth like a fish out of water.

'Look,' said Billy, 'you've got the wrong end of the stick. We're not interested in you. We need to ask you a question about *us*.'

'Yes,' I said, finally finding my voice. 'The thing is, could we go somewhere a bit more private? We don't want to talk to you in the street like this.'

'Surely,' said The Hurricane, and he looked a little

surprised. Perhaps he finally grasped that we were serious because he turned abruptly and crossed the street to a café. It was right by a guitar shop. In spite of everything, I noticed Billy's eyes lighting up. In the midst of all the drama he still had time for guitars.

At the café there were more spectators, but we felt less conspicuous because we were sitting down and closer together. Then The Hurricane put on his sunglasses and a baseball cap, which made him look more like a celebrity trying to hide. Of course this meant that people peered over at us and a waiter appeared instantly at our table. The Hurricane ordered. Billy said he wasn't thirsty and I continued to swig from the bottle of water to stop my throat from closing off altogether.

'Like I said,' said Billy, leaning closer to The Hurricane, 'we're here to talk to you about something important to *us*.' He emphasised the 'us' so that there could be no mistake.

'Yeah, yeah,' said The Hurricane, looking as if he'd heard every line in the book. 'Is it another blasted charity you want me to promote? A script you want me to read?'

'No. We don't want any of those things,' I said, my

teeth grinding together a little. 'We found your details – or rather we found Charles Ward's details – on an email attachment sent by fertility-whatsit.com and–'

'So you took a lucky guess and found out it was me? Gee, what a surprise!'

Harry Hodder just didn't let up. He was unstoppable. In Harry Hodder World all roads led straight back to him. But in real life they didn't and he needed to know that they didn't and I was going to tell him because I was sick of him talking over us and I'd just about had enough.

'No!' I said. 'I did not take a lucky guess. I had no idea Charles Ward was you. I really don't care if it *is* you. I don't even like your TV show. If you want the truth, I think that you're rude and obnoxious, but what I really want to know is – WAS IT YOUR SPERM THAT MY MUM GOT OFF THE INTERNET?'

I practically shouted that last bit. In fact, I fully admit that I did. And I became aware that the café had gone rather quiet. All polite chit-chat had ceased and everyone was staring at us.

A red glow crept up The Hurricane's neck. The blush surged towards his ears, which now stood out like flaming beacons on either side of his head.

'Erm . . . I'm sorry,' said The Hurricane. He was almost lost for words.

'That's OK,' I said. I did feel quite bad for drawing attention to us like that. But finally we were getting to the point. I held my breath.

'The thing is . . .' The Hurricane leaned forward and so did Billy and I, as did most of the people in the café. 'The thing is, it can't have been me.'

'Oh.' I said. I exhaled. I felt punctured. Deflated. Around us there was a perceptible sigh and then people began to chat normally again.

'Are you sure?' said Billy.

'Quite sure,' said The Hurricane. 'Absolutely certain. The thing is, I didn't go through with it.'

'Oh,' said Billy.

'Oh,' I said.

'The website got in touch,' continued The Hurricane. 'I guess it must have been on behalf of your mum. And I was going to do it, but then at the last minute I just couldn't. Didn't have the guts. When it came to the crunch, it was just too big a deal. So I bottled. I bailed. I didn't do it. I pulled out of the programme altogether.'

'Oh,' I said again. I became aware that I had a pain in

my jaw from where I'd been clenching it for the last twenty minutes.

'The guys that go through with it,' said The Hurricane, 'some of them are really courageous – I mean, they know what life is about. And now you're here and you're all disappointed. And I'm truly sorry.'

He did look sorry too.

'S'OK,' I said, although it didn't really feel OK at that precise moment. Billy put his hand on my arm.

'I'm truly sorry – I am,' said The Hurricane again. 'This was a misunderstanding and I hope you find your dad. I hope he's a really great guy. You deserve him to be.'

We sat for a moment in silence. Harry Hodder's shoulders had drooped. He looked like a tall, sad middle-aged man in a ridiculous baseball cap. You'd never guess he was a big TV star. Even though I was feeling pretty sorry for myself, I almost started to feel sorry for him too. What if he'd given me a different answer? What if he'd said, 'You can call me Dad!' Maybe it wouldn't have been so bad after all.

Then he flashed one of his famous Hurricane smirks at me and leaned in.

'Do me a favour,' he said. 'Don't spread this about, will you? I'll text you my agent's number. Any time you want tickets – anything – just give him a call. Lovely man, Dennis. Always happy to speak to my friends.'

Then the man who was not my dad stood up and walked off out of the café and down the street, pulling the peak of his cap low over his brow.

'*Be brave! Be brave!*' said Billy. 'Turns out the man's a total coward.' And he started to laugh, and after a while so did I. We both sat there laughing uncontrollably because the last half an hour had been so odd and because we had thought for one terrible moment that I shared half my genes with The Hurricane and it was good to laugh. I laughed until my eyes shed their tears quite freely down my cheeks and into my mouth. I suddenly wished Tony was there. Maybe, just maybe it would have been OK for him to see me cry.

I felt the vibration of a phone in my coat pocket. Charles Ward? Harry Hodder? But it turned out to be Mum. I didn't answer and switched off the old phone. There were three missed calls from her on my current phone too. I was guessing she was wondering where I was. Doing her usual nought-to-sixty hysteria. I knew we should think about heading home if we wanted to avoid awkward questions about our whereabouts.

'Let's make a pact,' I said to Billy, 'that we will never, ever take Harry Hodder up on his stupid, patronising ticket offer, even though your mum is obsessed with him.'

'Agreed,' said Billy. Even now I could see his gaze wandering over my shoulder to the shop next door.

He'd been great. He deserved a reward.

'Billy,' I said, 'we can go to the music store and look at the guitars now if you like.'

My cousin's smile practically split his face in two.

27

Anak

'Guitar strings,' we said to Uncle Zé and Aunt Lilah as we walked through the salon that evening. This was the explanation we'd come up with as to where we'd been for the last four hours. When your family's default setting is hysteria, then if you're five minutes late they imagine you've fallen over, cracked your head or worse. Four hours late means you've been raped, killed and eaten by dogs.

'Guitar strings,' said Uncle. 'Because we needed more guitar strings in this house. I was just saying to Lilah, "we run clean outta guitar strings, darling. I do hope Billy brings some when he gets back FROM MARS" or wherever it is you two *bobos* think you've been. It's half past seven!!'

Have you ever noticed that when parents want to emphasise how badly you've behaved, it generally comes down to what time it is?

'This bloke at school was selling strings,' said Billy unconvincingly. 'He had loads of them. I think he'd cleared out an old music shop or something.'

That line stank. It wasn't in the script we'd agreed on the way home.

'Oh, was he "selling strings"?' said Aunt Lilah. She was standing there brandishing a pair of curling tongs. She looked menacing. 'And where does "this bloke" live? The Shetland Islands?'

'No,' said Billy, 'he's just off Queensbridge Road actually.'

'Well, it's seven thirty and you've been to McDonald's,' said Uncle Zé.

'How do *you* know?' I said.

'Because you're holding a McFlurry, *chooch*.'

Oh yeah.

'And there *is* no McDonald's on Queensbridge Road,' said Aunt Lilah.

'Oh, we kind of went via Mare Street.'

'And we called you seven times,' said Aunt Lilah.

'Billy didn't have his mobile . . .'

'And your mother called you too and we don't like the two of you hanging around any old place after school unless we know where you are and who you're with.'

'Oh.'

'So DON'T DO IT!' bellowed Uncle Zé. '*Idyotas*.'

'Ok.'

'Your mother was very worried,' Uncle said to me.

'Sorry, *tito*.'

'I've had to do some calming down. She will be OK when I call her now, so no harm done.'

'But don't do it again!' said Aunt Lilah, and she stalked off holding the curling tongs, as if she wasn't afraid to use them on someone if they made a sudden movement that she didn't like.

'You come and have proper food now,' said Uncle. 'Oh and by the way, Billy, Tony is here. He's doing something with the guitar. Apparently there's a rehearsal tonight. First I heard of it.'

Uncle gave me a funny look when he said that about Tony. Then he went into the kitchen and we heard him turn on the rice cooker, and then we heard him start frying. This was generally a good sign because he enjoys frying.

Billy disappeared off to the bathroom. He hates being in trouble with anyone. It affects his stomach. I went on up to his room. Tony was there reading one of Billy's nerdy guitar mags.

'Hey,' he said. 'How'd it go?'

'I can't even begin to explain,' I said.

Because how do you explain that you've just spent half an hour believing your dad might be Harry Hodder and then realising that he wasn't? Anyway, I tried. Tony's eyes got rounder and rounder.

'No way, man,' he kept saying, his head nodding up and down wildly. 'I mean, seriously – that is crazy stuff.'

I told him the bit about the agent and the free tickets. Tony said, 'What a loser.'

Billy stuck his head round the door. 'Wossup?'

'Hurricane-Dad-Man,' said Tony. 'What a looooser.'

'He *was*,' said Billy. 'We didn't like him at all.'

I shook my head, 'I'm actually glad he's not my dad.'

'How'd you get on with the amp?' said Billy, and he began emptying his pockets of guitar strings and plectrums and cable ties and then he and Tony went into one of their geek-speaks and I tuned out.

'You all ready for tomorrow night?' I said eventually when they'd stopped whirring at each other, because it was Rock Dove's debut at The Forge and my possible prelude-to-a-date with Tony and my chance to style the band.

'All ready,' said Tony. 'Well, we have a rehearsal at eight-thirty tonight.'

'Ready as we'll ever be,' said Billy.

'Should be an awesome night,' said Tony, and he smiled at me, which was great and all, but after the experience I'd just had I wasn't entirely sure I could cope with any kind of awesomeness.

'I need to get home,' I said. 'I've had a freaky day. I need to be in my normal bed with my normal teddy.'

Plus I needed to cook up some ideas as to how to style the band. This was a big moment for me and I hadn't even had a chance to think about it.

'I'll walk you out then,' said Tony. 'That OK?'

It was more than OK.

Tony walking me out was not OK with Uncle Zé however. It was not OK at all. 'I thought you were staying for proper food, Sadie,' he said, and he came and stood at the kitchen door holding a spatula. I wondered where the need for my family to hold random household objects in a threatening manner had suddenly come from.

'I need to get back, *tito*,' I said. I didn't want to eat his good food right now. It clearly meant too much to him.

'Hmm.' He eyed me. 'You remember what I said, Sadie?'

'Yes, *tito*.' I blushed. He might as well have been standing there with a shotgun.

As soon as we got outside, Tony said, 'What the hell was all that about? We normally get on OK, but lately – *phew* – I don't know what's happened.'

'You walked me home,' I said.

'I walked you home?'

'You walked me home before and you're walking me home now.'

'Well, I don't know why you're searching for your dad, Sadie, cos it seems to me he's right here.'

I breathed in sharply. Even Tony could see it.

'You know what?' I said, 'That is *exactly* what I've been thinking.'

'How d'you mean?' said Tony, turning to face me, 'You don't mean . . .'

I nodded.

'Your *actual* Dad?'

I nodded again. It was only when I nodded that I realised that this *was* what I'd been trying not to think. That Uncle Zé just might be my real dad.

'Do you honestly think . . .?'

I nodded again.

'It'd be pretty out-there,' said Tony. 'I mean, your family seem like they're open with you about other stuff. You'd think they might . . . Are you sure? I thought stuff like this only happened in funny little places in America.'

'I don't really know where stuff like this happens,' I said. 'And no, I'm not sure. But it's not impossible, is it?'

'This is turning out to be quite a weird sort of day,' said Tony.

'Yes. I know.' I felt a great bubble of emotion rising through my chest and landing up just behind my eyes. Tears were coming. I didn't know whether to laugh or cry. I sniffed.

Tony put his arms round me. It was sort of instinctive and it felt OK to bury my head in his shirt.

'What if Uncle Zé really is my dad?' I murmured, my voice muffled by the soft cloth.

'But what about the computer files?' said Tony.

I'd already thought of that. I pulled away from his side and gazed up at him. He looked totally bewildered. 'Well, we know two of them didn't work out, so who's to say the third did?'

'But what about your mum's email to the website, announcing your birth?'

I'd thought of that too. 'It never actually said that she'd used a donor. It was like a 'thank you for your help and interest in making this happen' email. So maybe she just gave up. After all that searching that Aunt Lilah goes on about every single year . . .'

'And all along it was Uncle Zé.'

I left Tony at the corner of the road. He was shaking his head. He must have been finding it hard to be entirely positive about the situation for once. He looked forlorn and alone standing there, which was just how I felt.

As I walked the rest of the way home, different phrases and half-remembered conversations drifted through my memory:

There are no 'right guys' in my experience — well, your Aunt Lilah got him

Anak

You are all the daughter I need, Sadie

Anak

I bet you're really glad you don't have a dad, because one is enough

Anak

At home, after Mum had finished yelling at me for not telling her where I was, for not answering the phone and for being a general pain in the backside, I grabbed her laptop and escaped to my bedroom. I Googled a*nak* — the name that Uncle Zé had always called me. I knew what it meant. I just needed to see it written down.

Anak - Filipino for child or more accurately son or daughter.

I stared into the mirror. Black, straight hair. Olive skin. My eyes are the same shape as Mum's, but Billy and I could easily pass for brother and sister.

Oh, Uncle Zé — why didn't anybody tell me? Why had they been lying to me all this time?

And what the hell was Billy going to think?

Current Mood: anchorless

Groovechick2: who took ur anchor?

SayD: every1. My family. Feel unstable – think every1's bin lying 2 me

Groovechick2: bout wot?

SayD: bout my dad

Groovechick2: Y would they do that?

SayD: don't no

Groovechick2: 2 protect u?

SayD: praps

Groovechick2: ask em

SayD: can't jus ask em. Can I?

Groovechick2: SayD – be a grownup. Face up to em. U did it wiv the meangirlz. Do it wiv ur family if u think they lying 2 u. Just ask em

28

This is My Story

Friday 5th October
Hairstyle: Big Big Hair

This hairstyle is all about the teasing! It's a complete winner for parties as it's all about glam and voluminous waves that are thick, glossy and luxurious. Part off a section of hair from the rest and backcomb vigorously. Spray newly teased sections with a firm-hold hairspray. To make this style big and bold, use both hands to carefully smooth the teased hair back in the opposite direction, making sure there is volume in this area. You have lift. You have luxury. You know you look great!

If this was my cousin Billy De Souza's story — if it was Billy who was searching for his dad — then he'd stick with the facts because he is a Fact Man and that's what it always comes down to for him. He'd say, 'OK. So. We had three suspects and we eliminated two. So I conclude

259

that my Dad is number 241, Abraham Smith. And that's that. This has satisfied any curiosity I had regarding my genetic heritage for the time being and I feel I can move on to my next project. I don't need to meet Abraham Smith, although I do sometimes wonder if he has a guitar. And if he does, what type it is, man.'

If this was Shonna Matthew's story, she'd say something like this: 'I'm so angry with Mum for keeping all this stuff secret from me. Who the hell does she think she is? God? Well, I wanted to *show* her she can't pull the wool over my eyes. So I went for it. Met up with a couple of middle-aged guys who it turns out were completely minted. Of course, neither one was my dad, so it looks like it's the gardener, unless of course Mum's setting me up and it's Uncle Zé. In which case I AM REALLY REALLY SUPER MAD. AGGGGGGGHHHHHH!!!!!'

However, this was not Billy's story or Shonna's story. This was definitely my story and I had to find my own way through it, and currently, not based on any evidence at all, I had a gut feeling that I was being lied to. Uncle Zé was my Number 1 Dad-suspect now and everything else was looking like a smokescreen to cover this up.

Unfortunately it seemed that there was no way of proving this other than by direct confrontation, so this was the way I had to go. But really – if people had lied to me then what did they expect?

'I think I'm just going to come right out and confront my family this evening,' I said to Tony when we met up in the music lab that Friday lunchtime.

We were meant to be discussing my style plans for the band. We'd worked out that I would have precisely two hours between Friday night tea at Aunt Lilah's and the gig at The Forge. In this time slot I had to transform a group of five lads, one of whom favoured pointy boots and two of whom preferred oversized skate-wear, plus Tony (the post-rock jock) and Billy (geek-dressed-by-Mum) into something resembling a 'band'. They needed to be a cohesive unit, style-wise. It wasn't going to be easy. It was doubtful that it was even achievable, especially as it appeared to be no one's priority but Tony's. Billy had opted out of discussions in favour of restringing his guitar at home. I think he was getting me back for leaving him mid-style the previous Saturday. His text just said: **Rok Duv duz not = hair**

The rest of the band hadn't showed either. They

obviously thought you could make it to the top in their mix of bleached-out Metal T-shirts and baggy shorts or skinny black drainpipes and winkle pickers. So it was just me and Tony. Not that I minded. Our style plan was all black, as we figured that no one could object to this. Tony would wear a purple T-shirt so that he stood out as the lead singer and I would concentrate on styling their hair. The two-hour time slot would be a challenge. But this paled in comparison to the challenge of the Friday night tea beforehand.

'I've decided I'm going to say, "I have something to ask you all. Is Uncle Zé more than just my Uncle? Is he my donor? Is he my dad?"' I was being completely down to earth and practical about this. It was the only way.

'Woah,' said Tony, his head nodding like it was going to fall off.

I continued. 'Psychologically I think it's best to ask just as everyone's been served their main course. What do you think?'

'Jeez Louise – I don't know! I mean, there aren't really any rules about this stuff, are there?'

'I figure if I ask them at this stage, they'll sit there and their dinners'll be going cold, and Uncle can't stand food going cold – I mean, he really loses the plot over it. So then he'll just tell me the truth so they can get on and eat.'

'Woah,' said Tony again. 'Maybe. Your family is a lot different to mine. I think mine would forget the food with a line like that.'

My family would never just forget the food. My family is all about the food.

'The thing is, what if I'm wrong?'

I'd spent the last twelve hours fixating on the possibility that Uncle Zé might be my dad. I had talked myself into it. I was almost positive. He *was* my dad. It all fitted.

'This is a pretty rad course of action,' said Tony, his head pumping up and down. 'No matter what the outcome is – to just say it like that at the dinner table. Won't it kind of make everything awkward for everyone?'

'Awkward!' I practically shouted it. 'If they'd all had this conversation sixteen years ago then maybe I wouldn't be asking the "awkward" question now!' I breathed hard. 'Yes, it'll be a little difficult. Aunt Lilah will start shrieking, Uncle Zé will go and do some urgent frying, Billy'll restring his guitar for the zillionth time, Great Aunty Rita will shout, "What? If you'd sent her to Hillel Heights she'd never even have heard the word sperm!" and Mum'll go very quiet and teary.'

'And you?' said Tony, and he gently put his hands on my shoulders. 'What will you do, Sadie? What do you want out of this whole scenario?'

What *did* I want?

'I just want to know the truth,' I said.

Tony looked at me solemnly for a few moments. 'This is a really big deal,' he said eventually.

'I know,' I said. 'It's so intense I'm almost over it. Let's just go back to styling the band instead.'

29

Closing the Lid

From: Sadie.nat@cupcakedanceparty.com

Sent:Fri 5/10 12:26

To: abe.smith@kent.gov.uk

Subject: Last Call

Dear Abraham Smith

Hi

This is my last email to you. I haven't heard back from you,
but I haven't had an 'undeliverable' email back either, so
I'm guessing you've been receiving these but maybe you
don't want to respond because you know that it's not you
I'm after. I just want to say that's OK and sorry for bothering
you and all.

From

Sadie Nathanson

'More emails?' said Miss Frame. She'd been watching me from the far end of the library and now she was coming over to talk. 'Are you now having a full-scale correspondence with your dad?'

'Not really,' I said. 'It's more like I've got to close the lid on something.'

'OK . . .'

'I mean, I've worked it out for myself and I don't think I'm going to find my dad over the Internet.'

Miss Frame raised her eyebrows. 'And that's good, is it?'

'I dunno if it's good. It is what it is. I just need confirmation. I'm pretty sure I know who he is now.'

'If you know,' said Miss Frame, 'then why d'you need confirmation?'

'I guess I want to know why no one's told me the truth.'

'Why do you think they haven't told you the truth?' said Miss Frame. She patted her hair. She'd straightened it and curled it under and secured it with a neat little Alice band. It was so 1950s. It was so *her*. It was hard for me to concentrate on the conversation when someone's hair was that good.

'Sadie?'

'I guess they didn't want to upset me or something.'

'Which is a good enough reason maybe,' said Miss Frame.

She was right. It was a good enough reason. I mean look what happened sometimes when you did find out the truth; like when you sat in McDonald's and you realised that the old tramp sitting in the corner was your dad. Maybe sometimes it was better not to know.

I managed to avoid spending too much time at home after school. I didn't want a scene with Mum in case it completely threw me off my mission, which, in spite of my conversation with Miss Frame, I was still pretty sure I was going to go ahead with. I wanted to avoid my resolve being diluted further, plus my schedule was incredibly tight. It went something like this:

3.30–4 p.m. Get changed for the gig

4–5 p.m. Style Billy's hair at Aunt Lilah's

5–7 p.m. Tea and ask if Uncle Zé is my dad. Ask early and allow extra time for hysterics

7–9 p.m. Style rest of Rock Dove
9 p.m. Party/gig leading to possible my-first-date
with Tony

So I nipped home after school just long enough to get changed into my coolest I'm-with-the-band outfit, including spray-on jeans, stripy tee, hoop earrings and of course the Betty Boop Uggs. I reteased my Big Big Hair and piled on more spray. The style was holding well. Then I repacked my stylist's case complete with straightening irons, spray, gel (wet-look and super-hold), crazy colours (spray-ins) and even some hair extensions (well, who knew?). As I ran out of the flat, Mum came in. She was clutching a pile of post.

'Mail for you!' she shouted as I ran by. She was trying to use junk mail as an excuse for a mum-and-daughter moment. But it was going to take more than that to stop me.

'Gotta run!' I said. 'I'm doing everyone's hair. I'll see you at Aunty's.'

I went straight round to Aunty and Uncle's place. Billy was on the sofa polishing a fingerboard. He was to be my first style victim. Without saying anything, I beckoned him over to one of the kitchen chairs, put a towel round his neck before he could protest and started squirting water and combing fiercely.

'Watch the hair,' he said pointlessly.

'Oh, and how is my favourite great niece?' yelled Great Aunty Rita as she walked in, chuckling to herself.

'I'm fine, Aunty.' I went over and kissed her.

Uncle Zé popped his head round the door. He had his apron on and he held his arms out to me for a hug. 'We're having *Pork Belly and Rice – the Sequel,*' he said, 'to make up for your birthday when you ended up wearing it.'

'Thank you, *tito,*' I said.

'No pork for me,' said Great Aunty Rita.

'Chicken for Aunty Rita!' said Uncle. 'One day we'll convert you. Bring you over to our side.'

'Never,' said Great Aunty Rita. 'And how are you, my dear? How's school?'

'It's a car crash,' I said.

'Yes, dear,' said Great Aunty Rita. She was deaf or wasn't listening or something.

'But I'm fine, just fine.' I said. Because I was feeling just fine.

*

'Good hair, Billy,' said Mum a bit later when we all sat down for tea.

'You've done a good job on him actually, Sadie,' said Aunt Lilah. 'I'm impressed. You can sweep up for me any time!'

'Cheers,' I said.

Billy's hair *had* turned out well: side-swept fringe with waxed tips to keep them in place. I couldn't wait to get my hands on the rest of the band. I just had this small hurdle to get over first. Asking that question.

It was hard to pick a moment because everyone was looking really quite happy and what I was about to say was going to stop them looking like that. Uncle started going on again about the things he saw when he looked out of the window. Mum was saying that one of her almost bankrupt businesses was picking up – they'd even been able to pay her this week. Billy played us '50 Ways to Leave Your Lover' on the acoustic with no mistakes. Great Aunty Rita told us about her new bridge partner Harry Sherman who, at sixty-eight years old, was the youngest in the Redbridge Seniors Jewish Bridge League and who she referred to at a thousand decibels as 'my toy boy', and Aunt Lilah talked about a customer who wouldn't acknowledge his baldness and kept asking her for hairstyles which were increasingly impossible to achieve. Today it was dreadlocks.

I stared round the dinner table as they passed bowls backwards and forwards, gossiping and scolding and laughing about the week's events. They weren't really such bad people considering they were all I had. It wasn't so terrible that I'd ended up here, was it? Did I really need the last piece of the puzzle so badly that I'd risk wrecking it all?

'Look,' I said suddenly – but everyone carried on talking. I tried again half-heartedly. 'Look, I just . . .'

'I mean,' Aunt Lilah continued, 'what's a polite way of saying, "Sid, you're bald as a coot, love. I can give you three dreadlocks – one for every strand you have left on your head"?'

She was right. You had to match the style to the hair sometimes. Not the other way round. It just didn't work like that.

Mum put her hand on my arm. 'What did you want to say, love?'

And the room went quiet.

'I . . . I just wanted . . .'

I paused. They were all looking at me: Aunt Lilah, Mum, Great Aunty Rita, Uncle Zé and Billy. They were looking at me and smiling. They were smiling at me because they loved me. Because they were my family. The room swam in front of me, like it had on my birthday. I took a long deliberate breath in, just like Miss Frame did, conscious of my chest going up and down.

'I . . . I agree with you, about the hair, I mean. You can't give a man with three hairs dreadlocks. You can sell him a number 1 though. Find him a picture of Bruce Willis and tell him he has the same head shape and he'll totally go for it. And he'll look good.'

I'd just chickened out. I'd bailed. At the last moment I couldn't go through with it.

'Sadie's right!' said Aunt Lilah. 'And I will tell Sid, when the dreadlocks have grown out!'

It seems that I wasn't the only one who'd chickened out.

30

Shonna Matthews Was Nothing

I styled them. Totally. The entire band. Even the no-hopers who looked as if nothing would ever make them look remotely presentable. I straightened them and lacquered them and waxed them to within an inch of their sad little dweeb-boy lives. Styling Tony was OK though.

'So I'm guessing you didn't have the big confrontation scene,' he said, while I sprayed blue on to the tips of his fringe. 'I was worried about it. And are you giving me a blue rinse?'

'Don't talk – you'll get dye in your mouth.'

'Well? Did you?'

'No,' I said. 'I was about to and then I just didn't. Or couldn't. It felt all wrong. They don't deserve it – any of them. Whatever they did, they did it for a good reason and maybe I don't even want to know the truth. There. You're done now.'

273

Tony's hair looked cool and at that moment he stood up and kissed me – like properly. On the lips – a date-kind-of kiss. Then he looked in the mirror.

'You're great,' he said, 'and you're a great hairdresser.'

The crowd were beginning to arrive. Climbing the steep steps to The Forge, they tumbled in and the sound system cranked up and we found ourselves in the middle of a party. It was only when Rock Dove took to the stage and played their first number that I became conscious of the big grin plastered across my face, which for the life of me I just couldn't wipe off. It was about Tony and it was about my family and it was about being a good hairdresser too.

I glanced away from the stage and back into the crowd. Shonna Matthews was standing there on her own. Imelda was nowhere in sight. Shonna Matthews who had started this whole thing in the first place by sending me that phony Dadcard. If she turned around and smiled at me now, it would be OK, but it wouldn't mean like *everything*. I was over her. She was nothing.

I just had to share the love. All of it. Groovechick2 was the obvious candidate so as soon as I got home, I grabbed Mum's laptop and went online to hunt her out.

Current Mood: idiot grin

Groovechick2: & & &?
SayD: we kissed
Groovechick2: and ur dad?
SayD: chickened out of asking but don't really mind
Groovechick2: and meangirlz?
SayD: all gone
Groovechick2: u got the power

31

An Actual Printed Letter

Mum opened the lounge door just as I closed the laptop. Dammit. She'd waited up for me. She was wearing her dressing gown and rubbing her eyes. I wondered if I was in trouble. For being late. For having anything that resembled a private life.

I decided to apologise in advance. Get it over with. I was too tired to argue, plus I was still on a high from Tony's kiss. Did it show? Could you tell?

'Sorry, I know I'm a bit late. How come you're up?' I said.

'I watched a movie,' said Mum.

She wasn't shouting or hysterical, although she did seem a bit agitated. She pulled an envelope from her pocket and thrust it into my hand. 'This came for you this morning – I tried to give it to you earlier. Looks personal. I thought it might be a late birthday card.'

Why hadn't she just left it on the table for me? Just

seemed like an excuse to stay up – to spy on me.

I turned the envelope over to open it. On the flap it said: Abraham Smith, 17 Weald Lane, Bough Beeches, Kent.

Oh. My. God. I took a sharp breath in.

'You OK?' said Mum.

'I just . . . I just need to . . . Just hold on there,' I said. I backed out of the room and went into the bathroom clutching the letter. I bolted the door, sat down on the edge of the bath and ripped open the envelope, my hands shaking uncontrollably.

Dear Sadie

Thank you for your emails. I realised in the last few days that I've never really understood the true meaning of the word 'surprise'. When I got your first email I had to go outside and walk around to try and take it all in. By the time I got the second one I'd just about figured out how I was going to answer. But I wanted to write it down, not email it. This felt like a moment to write a letter. I have two goats outside my house and I showed them this letter and one of them tried to eat it. I don't really know what to say so I'm following your Miss Frame's advice and writing like we're having a conversation.

Sadie — yes, I did offer to donate via a website and your mother contacted me, although I never found out if the donation was successful. But I'm guessing from your letter that it was.

I am <u>pleased and amazed</u> that you've contacted me. <u>Pleased and amazed</u>. But you should show this letter to your mother or father because they need to know that we've corresponded.

I would love to hear from you again, Sadie, because you sound like a brave and interesting young woman, but I will be content with the emails for the time being. They're extremely precious to me.

Abe Smith

And there was his mobile number, inviting me to call him up and speak to him.

I breathed out like Miss Frame, very slowly and deliberately. I put the letter down and went to the window above the sink, opened it and took in a lungful of cold evening air. I felt dizzy. I felt hot and then cold. Then I read the letter again. And again. Poring over every word, every full stop.

*

When I finally came out of the bathroom, Mum was standing there looking worried.

'Everything all right, love?' she asked. 'I thought–'

'Mum – the letter,' I said, because the news was bursting out of me. 'It's from . . .'

'I know,' said Mum. 'I know who it's from, love. I knew when I saw the name.'

She said it very calmly and quietly, her pale blue eyes were totally clear. There were no tears. She held out her arms to me and we hugged like we hadn't done in the longest time.

'Mum,' I said, 'please don't say anything to anyone yet – I mean Aunt Lilah and Uncle Zé and all.'

She looked at me slightly quizzically. It was almost as if she didn't understand the idea of privacy.

'Can we just keep this between us – just for now? Let me decide who to tell and when.'

She nodded at me and then hugged me again.

'Sadie, I'm in shock,' she said. 'I don't know what to say. I've imagined this moment for a long time, but I imagined it all wrong. It didn't quite go like this.'

'How did it go?'

'When I made the decision to have you the way I did, of course I knew that there would be a moment like this and . . . it's a very wonderful moment. I just assumed that we'd do it together. But I'm guessing you went ahead and found your father on your own . . .'

'Mum, you just wouldn't listen. I did try to ask you about it.'

'*I* wouldn't listen?'

'No. There was always something else going on.'

Mum looked at me. She sighed and shook her head. 'I wouldn't listen.'

'So I had to find him without you. I did it with Billy. Billy and I found him – Abraham Smith – we found him together.'

Mum went towards the window. She stood looking out for what felt like a really long time.

'I'm listening now,' she said eventually, 'so you'd better tell me what you want to do.'

32

Lucky

Saturday 6th October

Hairstyle: Bed Head

This is a style to relax into. Towel your hair dry and add mousse or gel to the ends. Scrunch-dry under a diffuser. It'll look cute and tousled. Add a bow for a super-sweet effect. You'll look as if you got out of bed on the right side!

The next morning I felt as if I was waking up in a beautiful dream. My lips were still tingling from Tony's kiss and my hand was clutching Abe's letter. My donor's letter. My *dad's* letter. I leaped out of bed buzzing with excitement, like a kid on Christmas morning, and then I did something I hadn't done in the longest time. I knocked on Mum's door and, hardly waiting to hear her moans of, 'Oh God, it's Saturday!' I marched in and got into her bed.

'Mum,' I said, 'can we please call him?'

Mum didn't answer for a moment. She turned over and peered at me. 'You want to call Abraham Smith now?' she said.

I nodded.

'It's a little early,' she said. 'I mean, it's quarter to seven on a Saturday.'

'Oh.'

'Do you actually want to get him out of bed?'

'Yes! Yes!' I was so excited that I didn't care what time of day it was.

'Well, give it three more hours and then call. And even then it's pretty early for a Saturday. When you're being normal, Sadie, you do actually know this.'

She started to slide back under the duvet. I bit my lip. I didn't think I could wait three more hours.

'Will you do it with me, Mum?'

She smiled at me. Her face had red marks on it where it had been pressed into the pillow. The front of her hair had its habitual fluffed-up look and the back . . . well, it was long and lank, another hairstyle entirely.

A thought struck me: what was the best way of usefully passing three hours? What was the best way I knew to distract myself from whatever was going on in my life?

'Mum,' I said, 'can I cut your hair?'

I decided on a stacked bob. Simple, classic and flattering to all face shapes. I layered out the top, gradually going from the shortest fluffs that Aunt Lilah had been cutting in for the last thirty-odd years, to longer and longer layers. At the back I took away those long strands and cut sharply into the nape at an angle, creating fullness and softening Mum's jawline. At the front I kept the layers longer, creating a side parting and shaping the short bits into a wispy fringe.

By eight thirty that Saturday morning my mum was sporting One Presentable Hairdo for the first time in her forty-eight years and she seemed pleased with it.

'You know what, Sadie, you did a good job. How am I going to tell Lilah I have a new hairdresser?'

'The thing is, Mum, Aunt Lilah has always given you the hairstyle you wanted,' I said tactfully. 'It's just that you wanted the wrong one and luckily, this morning, I've been able to give you the right one. The one you didn't even know you wanted.'

'Well, I like it.'

'Well, you must look after it,' I said. 'Don't let it grow too long and get ratty and split – this is a salon hairdo and it needs to be kept in check by a pro.'

'OK,' she said, 'you win. I surrender.'

I was practising my spiel on her – the one I'm going to use on my customers when I have my own salon. For the next hour, every time Mum passed a mirror, I noticed how she gazed quickly at her hair and lifted her hand to it and moved a strand this way and that.

The hair was a great diversion, but by nine thirty I'd almost worn a hole in the carpet from pacing and Mum was on to her fourteenth cup of coffee. By nine forty-five I couldn't stand it any longer.

'Can we please call him now?'

'Well, OK,' said Mum, 'but it is still very early for a Saturday.'

'He's a gardener,' I said. 'He'll be up.'

'Possibly. Or perhaps this is the one morning he has a lie-in.'

'He'll be up.'

*

284

And he was up. Sort of.

My hand shook slightly as I dialled the number. Mum was sat right next to me and she squeezed my knee encouragingly.

'Hello?' said a man's voice. It was faintly husky — like he'd just got up. Then he cleared his throat and said 'Hello?' again a bit clearer.

I sat with the phone frozen to my ear in 'Dad-shock' — the state I seemed to find myself in when about to speak to someone who might be my dad. All moisture had left my mouth and my tongue was dry and sticky.

'Say something!' whispered Mum, and tried to grab the receiver from me. This propelled me into action.

'Hi,' I said, 'this is Sadie Nathanson.'

There was a pause. And then, 'Sadie! Hi! This is Abe!' said Abraham Smith. He sounded really friendly. I was immediately relieved and relaxed slightly.

'Oh good,' I said. 'I was hoping . . .'

'How are you? I'm so glad you got my letter because I got your last email and I was worried you'd given up on me.'

'Yuh — I got the letter yesterday, thanks.'

285

'This is pretty exciting,' said Abe, 'and a bit surprising. In a good way.'

'Yeah. It's a surprise all right,' I said.

'You found me.'

'Yes, well, me and Billy – he's my cousin – we found you. We traced you through the website and you still have the same email.'

'I still have the same email,' said Abe. 'I'm still here. It's good to talk to you, Sadie. It's nice to hear your voice because I've been thinking about you since I got the first email.'

'Me too,' I said.

I wanted to say that I'd always been thinking about him, but that didn't seem quite right somehow because the person who I'd been thinking about was 'my dad', and this person on the end of the phone was Abe Smith, and I hadn't met him yet. I didn't know what kind of person he was or what he looked like or anything.

So we just chatted on a bit about where he lived and where I lived, and he said that we should meet sometime, and then he asked me, 'Do your mum and dad know you've contacted me because I think . . .' and there he was asking me about my dad, and it was so strange to hear him say that.

'There's just my mum and she's right here,' I said. 'Do you want to speak to her?'

He said he would and so I passed the phone over. Mum was looking red in the face and tense, and then I left the room because this bit was nothing to do with me.

I went into my bedroom and stared at my reflection in the mirror and thought about the amazing fact that the man I'd just been speaking to on the phone was half of my genes and quite possibly resembles me in some way that my mum doesn't. I've always said that I don't have a problem with the unusual way I came into this world, but now that I'd spoken to Abe Smith, I felt something more than just indifference about it. I felt truly lucky to have been given a life where there was a moment like this one.

33

A Pair of Hands Like Mine

Hairstyle: Evening Sophistication
You will be amazed at what a few rollers will do for your hair. I can't think of a better style for a night on the town! It will look as though you spent hours at the salon.

Sunday was going to be a landmark day for me and I needed matching landmark hair, so it seemed appropriate to go back to my actual birthday for hair inspiration. After all, my birthday was when this whole dad thing had started. Plus I'd never got to try out that hairstyle.

I set my alarm for 6.00 a.m., brushed and spritzed my hair and carefully put in the correct sized rollers according to the diagram. By midday I was sprayed, sophisticated and still smiling.

'This is a pretty dramatic moment for us,' said Mum as we passed the sign announcing two miles to Bough Beeches – our destination and Abraham Smith's home.

We hadn't told anyone where we were going. Mum had been fairly reserved throughout the journey. I'd put it down to the fact that she was driving outside of London along unfamiliar, winding country lanes. She certainly hadn't done nearly as much swearing as she usually does behind the wheel. And she hadn't cried once. Even when we got lost, she just said, 'This is it then, Sadie, hey? Are you OK, love?'

'I'm fine, Mum. You?'

'Yup – OK. Surprisingly. We're both OK then. Bit nervous, but that's to be expected and he sounded nice on the phone and in his letter. Should be fine. That's fine. We're just fine.'

Once or twice she gripped my hand. I think it was supposed to be comforting, but it felt a bit like she was clinging on. Poor Mum. She was trying so hard to make this my moment, but she was actually allowed feelings as well. We parked outside 17 Weald Lane. We'd passed mansions along the road and pretty pink cottages with roses round the door, but number 17 was a small, plain kind of house, standing on its own large plot and set right back from the road.

'This is it,' said Mum.

I blew the air out of my lungs and marched purposefully up to the front door. There was a doorbell which made a *cuckoo* sound when I pressed it. It made me smile. And I was still smiling when he opened the door.

Abraham Smith had brown wavy hair in a sort of non-style. Brown hair, olive skin and dark eyes. He was average height and build and he didn't appear to have a worry crinkle. He'd changed a bit since the Winston-Churchill-Baby photo. But hadn't we all?

It was actually his hands that made me know that we were related. They were small like mine. And stubby. And sort of dirty and weathered. Except that the dirt on his hands was soil and not ink or hair dye.

'Look,' I said, 'you've got my hands.'

Abe put his hands on the table and I put mine next to his.

'She's right,' said Sarah, Abe's girlfriend. 'She's got your hands or you've got her hands.'

'I had them first,' said Abe and he smiled at me.

His hands had stopped shaking by then. When I first walked through the door I couldn't help noticing that his hands were shaking. I couldn't help noticing because mine were too. He seemed calm enough – offered us tea and biscuits, told us to call him Abe, showed us his new Labrador puppy called Daisy – but when he held his cup of tea his hands shook so much that he had to put the cup down on the table.

'I'm nervous actually,' he said.

No kidding.

'Well, let's do something,' said Mum when we'd had a cup of tea, 'as we're all a bit nervous. Let's go look at your garden.'

Mum seemed so calm. In fact, she was Queen Serenity herself. Seeing as this was a big moment for her too, she was holding up surprisingly well. Not even close to hysteria.

The garden was a good suggestion. Abe seemed much happier outdoors. He completely relaxed, showed us all the plants, the fruit trees, the pond. Then he led us through a little rickety gate and into a walled field. The ground as far as you could see was covered in white flowers.

'Meadow saffron,' he said, 'also known as autumn crocus, and this is sea holly.'

I peered round at Mum. I don't think I've ever seen my mum in a garden in my life. She looked like she wasn't entirely sure what to do in it. But you just had to admire it. It looked as if it had been snowing in Abe's field – we were ankle-deep in the white flowers.

'This is beautiful, Abe,' said Mum. 'You've really got something special here, y'know.'

'Thanks,' said Abe. 'Glad you like it. What's it like where you live, Sadie?'

'It's not like here,' I said, because really it was the opposite. 'We live in a flat for one thing – we're just not very outside-type people, are we, Mum?'

Mum looked thoughtful – possibly not thoughtful: it was a look I didn't fully understand.

She turned to Abe. 'You do know that this was all Sadie's idea, don't you? She found you all on her own.'

Abe nodded.

'She's pretty resourceful, our daughter.'

It was so odd hearing my mum saying those words – 'our daughter'. It took my breath away and I blushed. Abe didn't though.

'You're right,' he said to Mum, and then he turned to me. 'You are pretty resourceful. And it took quite a bit of courage too, to do what you did. I'm in awe.'

I looked at Abraham Smith and my mum and I knew just where I'd got my courage from. They must have had it in spades to do what they did, too.

'You seem pretty smart to me as well,' said Abe, lightening the mood. 'What are you into? I mean, what are your interests?'

Sometimes grown-ups can ask you stuff like that, but they're just, y'know, making conversation. The odd thing about this question was that Abe sounded as if he actually wanted to know.

'Hair mainly,' I said, 'and style.'

'Great.'

'I mean, I don't just want to cut hair – I want to have my own salon and do really original styles, and interesting clients and a fancy interior designer do the salon out with amazing chairs and designery taps on the sinks. And all the stylists would be modelling the hair and we'll especially champion short hair for women.'

Then I gave him my theory about women with short hair. He looked as if he was really listening. I noticed Abe's girlfriend had come to join us in the garden and she instinctively grabbed on to her ponytail when I gave the haironomics lecture, like I was coming at her with the scissors already. Actually, she could easily wear a geometric bob – that's what I'd do for her.

'Wow,' said Sarah, 'you sound like you've got a plan there, Sadie.'

'Yeah, you've got it all figured out,' said Abe.

'Sadie has always had it figured out,' said Mum, but for once she wasn't being sarcastic. I recognised her expression now. She looked proud.

'You're lucky,' Abe said to me, 'because I'm thirty-seven years old and I still don't have any of it figured out.'

He was definitely Abe in my head now. He wasn't 'donor' or 'Dad #241' any more.

It's odd what you find when you go looking.

I went looking for my dad and what I found was a pair of hands that looked just like mine that belonged to a man who was not Dad, but who was half my genes.

The other thing I found was a strong and unexpected impulse to share him with the important people in my life. I could hardly wait to introduce him to Billy and Tony, but I also wanted him to meet Aunt Lilah, Uncle

Zé and Aunty Rita. Maybe he could even come over for Friday night dinner at some point.

Abe has eyes like mine and his hair is dark. Come to think of it he could really carry a buzz cut. I wonder if he'd let me do his hair . . .